DENNIS LOYNES was born in 1949 and has spent his whole life in the rural splendour that is Worcestershire. He retired from his job as Finance Director of a small group of motor dealers in 2008. He loved his job and is enjoying his busy life of retirement even more. He achieved an honours degree in Social Science in 2013 and discovered the thrill of writing by chance when crafting a Christmas story for his grandchildren. The solitary story grew and grew and became *Santa's Challenges* and the children's story was published in 2018.

In 2013 he had short stories published in *Figures in the Mist* and *Windmills and Paper Boats*. His first novel *Trials of Love* was published in 2017 by SilverWood Books. Since then, one thought kept flicking through his mind – what happened to the main characters in that book? Did things work out well for Paula and Beverley in particular? Did they find love? There was only one way to find out, and that's how *Pathway to Love* was born.

Dennis is a member of the Worcester Writers Circle and when not writing, loves tennis, badminton, jogging, Manchester United and duplicate bridge.

To find out more please visit www.dennisloyneswriter.com

G000128490

Also by Dennis Loynes

Trials of Love
Santa's Challenges

Pathway to Love

DENNIS LOYNES

SilverWood

Published in 2020 by SilverWood Books

SilverWood Books Ltd
14 Small Street, Bristol, BS1 1DE, United Kingdom
www.silverwoodbooks.co.uk

ISBN 978-1-78132-953-5 (paperback)
ISBN 978-1-78132-954-2 (ebook)

British Library Cataloguing in Publication Data
A CIP catalogue record for this book is
available from the British Library

Page design and typesetting by SilverWood Books

PATHWAY TO LOVE

Prologue

Paula

Light was beginning to push the darkness away as I approached the roundabout. I was in a different world, focusing on the morning ahead. I slowed but was roused into full alert by a bang that jolted me forward in my seat. "What the…?"

I got out and looked at the damage through the red mist that had descended. My Audi TT had been a gift from my parents on my eighteenth birthday; it was my pride and joy. Now there was a serious dent in the back and in my temper. A man about my age appeared from his car, bending to brush his hands against the broken paint on his vehicle before moving towards me, his arms raised in mock surrender.

"I didn't think you would stop. There was nothing coming," he protested.

"I need some details from you. NOW!" My voice was controlled and icy cold. I searched in my bag, took out my mobile phone, and quickly took photos of the scene. Cars were skirting around us, beeping their horns, accompanied by angry glares from the drivers. I looked hard at the information he gave me, passed him my insurance details, and exchanged telephone numbers before driving off.

I was quarter of an hour late when I arrived at work, and had to drive round and round before eventually locating a parking spot, which I managed to manoeuvre into. It should have been no surprise to me when I dirtied my clothes trying to escape from the small opening between my door and the car next to me. By the time I sat at my desk I was ready to explode, and I ignored all the stares from my fellow workers. They were used to me being first there in the morning and hard at work when they arrived.

I looked up to see my boss Colin gazing down at me. "I've never known you late before, what happened?"

I told him about the idiot driving into the back of me.

"Um, sorry about your car," he said with a gentle smile. "I know it means a lot to you."

Even in my wound-up state I noticed just a hint of uncertainty as he continued. "Come into my office when you're ready – there's someone I want you to meet. Bring your coffee with you."

Colin had been like a second father to me. Well, third, really, to be precise, but that's another story. I gathered up my notebook and pen and, a few minutes later, knocked on his door and entered. Colin was leaning back in his chair, his portly stomach thrust forward. I could see that the man opposite him was well dressed, even though he had his back to me, and the upright posture in his chair told me that this was serious.

Colin stood up and held out his hand. "Paula, I'd like to introduce you to Simon. Simon, this is Paula."

I had not seen the man before, but immediately I felt his eyes boring deeply into mine. Something about it disturbed me.

"So, you're the young lady I've heard so much about," he said.

I turned to Colin, trying to understand what this meeting was all about, but the face that was usually clear and decisive showed only apology. "Simon's taking over from me."

Although I didn't realise it at the time, within the space of a little over an hour, I had met the two people who would dominate my life over the years to come.

Chapter 1

Paula

I said that Colin had been my third 'father', a statement I should explain. My true or biological father died when I was just seven. He committed suicide when he learnt that his lung cancer could only have one long, drawn-out, painful conclusion. My mother tried to lessen our hurt by explaining that he chose this answer to an impossible question, as he loved my sister Beverley and me so much that he didn't want us to witness his suffering. He didn't want us to remember him that way, rather than the healthy, loving father that he had been.

Mum died too, just one year later when she was driving back from Malvern and her car suffered a blowout. Beverley and I were passed briefly to my grandparents, but they couldn't cope with two loud, boisterous girls. That was when my second parents came on the scene: Matt and Emily. I love them dearly; they could not have been better guardians. Though in all honesty, I did not always think of them so lovingly. I knew Matt from when my mum left me with him sometimes when she had meetings in Malvern, and I cannot remember any time when I felt anything but love for him. With Aunt Emily, however, it was different. At first, I saw only that she was taking the place of my real mum and I reasoned that it would have been sinful of me to forget Mum so easily and pass my affections on to her substitute. I shudder when I think how unpleasant I was in those early days. Distant, uncommunicative, shouting, storming out of the room when asked to do something. Then came that day at school when a girl in my class, Janice Bell, had laughed and baited me because my uniform was too small, as I stupidly refused to give it up as my mum had bought it for me. There had been a fight, which strangely had brought Aunt Emily and me together. She bared her soul about her own school days, and for the first time I didn't think of her as someone who had an easy, trouble-free life, with everything passed to her on a platter.

Then came the Davieses. But more about that despicable lot later.

Colin had come on the scene after I had left university and was keen to start on my career ambition of working in investment management. Matt, because of his work as a freelance accountant assisting local businesses, knew everyone in the community and had lots of connections everywhere. He also knew of my ambitions workwise, and I insisted that he should not use his influence to get me a job. I was determined to stand on my own two feet, a trait that Matt said I had inherited from Mum.

Colin's "Simon's taking over from me" had come like a bolt out of the blue.

"Where are you going then, Colin?" I wasn't able to stop myself from asking the question.

"I'm retiring, putting my feet up, taking things easy. My wife insists 'it's about time too'. I'll help Simon settle in until the end of the month, and then I shall slip quietly away."

I returned to my desk, concerned and worried. What a morning, and it was still only 9.30am. Yes, I was pleased for Colin, but I would miss him because he had always been there with a sympathetic smile when things went wrong. Full of sound advice delivered in a way that didn't make me feel like I was stupid, without a clue as to what I should be doing, though I still didn't know if Matt had coerced him into giving me a job and looking after me. Having said that, I was delighted that he was able to retire and enjoy life, but it didn't stop me feeling uncertain and vulnerable. There was something about Simon's gaze today that made me feel uncomfortable. What it was, I didn't know, but I had a feeling I would soon find out.

I went home to my flat that evening and cooked myself a pasta dish, but my thoughts were miles away thinking about work when my phone rang.

"Is that Paula Carter?"

I struggled to recognise the voice but failed. "Who's calling?"

"We met briefly this morning in, how I shall put it, unfortunate circumstances."

Now I recognised the voice. It was that driver from this morning, the one who'd gone into the back of me. "What can I do for you, Mr Brown?"

"I just wanted to say how sorry I am for what happened."

"Fine. You've done that, now thank you and goodbye." My finger went for the 'end call' button.

"Wait, don't go." He paused. "I wondered if I might buy you a meal as a way of saying sorry?"

I couldn't believe it. "Are you saying that because you drove into the back of me, you think I should go on a date with you?"

"I wouldn't put it quite like that."

"NO!" I ended the call and slammed the phone down on the table.

I was still seething with anger and indignation when the phone rang again. This time I was really going to give him a piece of my mind. "Yes?" I snarled, not checking whose number had flashed up on the screen.

"Wow, you don't sound that happy to hear from me." It was the gentle, loving tones of Uncle Matt.

"Sorry, Uncle Matt. It's not been the best of days. I didn't mean to snap at you."

"It's not like you,' he agreed. 'What's gone wrong?"

"Oh, everything. I'll tell you about it when I see you next."

"In that case, how do you fancy some Aunt Emily special cuisine tomorrow night? There's a chance Beverley might be around for a change and Harry would be really pleased to see you."

We chatted some more and as always I felt much happier after speaking to Uncle Matt. He had this reassuring quality that never failed to comfort me.

Chapter 2

Jason

'Bang' was the sound as my beaten-up old car collided with the one in front. I got out, hands raised in acceptance of my culpability. She looked at me in disgust. Not uncontrollable anger, nor steaming vitriol; it was cold, ruthless, and steely. Immediately she slipped into efficiency mode, her phone was pointed at the damage, then at my number plate. Insurance details and phone numbers exchanged, and then she was gone. Wow, I thought, she's something special.

I decided to phone her and apologise, but it wasn't a huge success.

"NO," she had shouted, before cutting me off abruptly.

So much for my less-than-subtle attempt to see her again. Even if I did, it seemed that I would only be viewed as a 'dent' in her day. Then when I went to hand my car into the Bodyshop repairer I saw an Audi TT gleaming back at me. I checked the registration number; it was hers – now dent-free. I had this brilliant idea and arranged for flowers to be placed on the passenger seat. On the card I left with it, I once more tendered my apology and hoped that she could eventually forgive my carelessness. I had to get on friendly terms with her, but how?

Chapter 3

Paula

As soon as I set foot inside the door, I was met by a big beaming smile from my step-brother Harry. "Sister Paula," he said excitedly. "Can I show you my new computer game? It's called Plants vs Zombies."

"After dinner, Harry love. You can show me all the bits and pieces of the game then. I'll look forward to it."

I knew that for Aunt Emily and Matt, Harry would always be thought of as a gift from God. When she found she was pregnant, Emily was nervous and apprehensive rather than excited and joyful. It was then that she told Beverley and me that she had suffered two miscarriages in the past. It was clear she believed there was a strong possibility that she would suffer further agony and heartache with no baby at the end of it. But baby there was. A healthy and lovely boy – Harry.

Beverley and I loved him from day one. Looking back, I can see that in a curious way he was the missing link that held the family together.

One day when Harry was only six, he casually asked me, "Why do you always call Mum 'Aunt Emily'?"

It was such an obvious question, but the affectionate name had been around for so long that no one noticed it any more. So, I told Harry about Bev's and my background. Harry simply shrugged. "Oh, okay." But from that moment on, it was always Sister Paula, or Sister Bev.

We all settled down to enjoy Aunt Emily's coq au vin, chatting merrily away, interrupting one another at will. All except Matt, who was worryingly quiet. I knew what that meant, so there was no surprise when he asked, "So what went so badly wrong with your day yesterday, that is, when I phoned?"

I sighed. Where to start? "Well, first of all some idiot drove into the back of me. Fortunately I've been able to get a loan car otherwise commuting to Birmingham would have been a nightmare. But then, wait for it, this same imbecile had the nerve to phone me up, under the pretence of apologising, and ask me out on a date."

"Really?" said Beverley, her eyes full of interest. "That gives a whole new meaning to 'hitting on you'."

I felt in just the right mood to smack her. She started to grin. Then the grin turned to laughter. Very quickly I was clutching my sides with laughter, too. I can never resist Bev's infectious laugh.

"I don't see what you're getting at," said Matt with concern. "Driving into the back of your car is hitting you, not hitting on you, and it's no laughing matter."

"Oh Dad, get with it. Hitting on you means someone fancies you," explained thirteen-year-old Harry. "What century are you living in?"

"'Making a pass' in your language," laughed Emily.

"I know, I know," lied Matt, trying unsuccessfully to deflect the ridicule.

"Did you say 'yes'?" asked Bev.

"Did I heck!"

It was after the dishes had been cleared away, when Uncle Matt casually mentioned, "I heard a rumour about Colin leaving. Is it true?"

I sighed. "It is. He's retiring."

"Well, I guess he's earned it. Who's taking over?"

"Simon. Simon Roach. From Somerset." I tried to sound non-judgmental, but Matt was too canny not to pick up the vibes.

"What is it? You don't like him, do you?"

"There's something about him," I replied. "I can't put my finger on it. It's just the way he looks at me; it makes me feel like I don't want to be there."

"Do you mean…" He searched for the right words.

I interrupted. "No, it's not a sex thing. His eyes just pierced straight through me, picking up what I was thinking. It makes me feel really uncomfortable."

Matt was quiet.

"Don't worry,' I said. 'It's probably just me. Perhaps it's because Colin was more of a mentor than a boss. I was always going to compare his successor unfavourably to him. I just need to come to terms with it."

"Simon Roach? You said he came from Somerset. I'll see what I can find out about him."

Exasperation took over. "Uncle Matt, I know you mean to be helpful, but there's nothing sinister. He's not Colin, that's all."

I joined Colin and Walker Investments five years ago not long after leaving university with an honours degree in business studies. I applied for a job there, and surprise, surprise, I got it. I often thought that Matt had used his vast network of business contacts to influence things, though he always denied it.

Colin Walker had founded his Birmingham company twelve years ago with a never-bending philosophy. First came the customer, second the employee and last the company. Unlike most investment companies it wasn't all about maximising the billing at every opportunity. Consequently, clients trusted Walker Investments and the database grew and grew.

There was a small staff of twenty and everyone worked hard. I knew that before I started. But I listened closely to the advice and criticisms and learnt quickly. Within eighteen months I had my own clients.

Now Colin was leaving.

Chapter 4

Jason

I phoned my friend and after getting an update on our local football team, I told him how I had stupidly driven into the back of a sports car.

"Much damage?" came the response.

"No, but she was definitely not happy. Not that anyone would be, but she is certainly not a person to cross."

My friend laughed.

It was a week later that I drove into Birmingham and wandered around aimlessly while waiting to collect my repaired car. I was standing outside a building with the plaque Walker Investments on the door wondering how to waste more time when a figure came rushing out and hurried across the road into a café.

The person looked familiar then I realised it was the girl from my car faux pas. I followed the smart businesslike figure, without a clue what I was going to say to her. I watched, hovering, as Paula went to the counter and placed her order.

She turned and stared at me with distaste. "Just when I thought my day couldn't get any worse, I bump into you."

"You've been crying?"

Her eyes were red and puffy. "So, what's it to you? You've already caused me grief. I thought it's what you did best."

"I'm sorry. I hate to see anyone unhappy. Particularly if it's

18

someone I like, and you seem a good person. Do you want to talk about it?"

She started to walk away.

"I know you're in a hurry. Let me buy you a coffee? It might help if you talk and share it."

I watched her dither and quickly placed an order before she could say no.

We found a seat and I tried to encourage her. "Tell me about it. Why has your morning been so bad?"

Her eyes filled with tears. "It's not just this morning. It's not been the same since Colin left. Simon hates me." She sobbed, but self-consciously brought her cup to her lips when she saw customers looking across at her.

"Why? I'm guessing Simon is your boss, or someone important? What makes you think he hates you?"

"Oh yes, he's my boss alright. Yesterday he had me making tea for him and this morning, in front of everyone, he asked me…no he didn't, he *told* me to get his sandwiches for him. He's taken over my two major clients himself and left me with the piddly little ones. He doesn't trust me and demeans me at every opportunity."

"What about everyone else? How does he treat them?"

"Oh, fine. It's only me he's got it in for."

"Do you have any friends there you can talk to? Unburden yourself, sort of thing?"

She looked nervously at her watch. "What? No, I'm too busy. Look, thanks for listening to my woes. It was wrong of me to bore you with my troubles. And thanks for the coffee." She picked up the sandwiches.

"Wait! Perhaps we can meet up again and talk things through? Your work problems, I mean." I felt her eyes look into mine for the first time.

"I'm sorry, you've been very patient, and I've definitely

19

misjudged you, but I'm not into relationships just now."

"I'm not talking about anything serious, just dinner and a chat."

"Maybe. Oh, and thank you for the flowers, it was a nice thought." Her laugh caressed my ears as she gazed at me. Then, she left.

Chapter 5

Paula

Strangely, I felt more at ease with myself, more settled, when I returned to work. Even the "bit of a queue was there?" followed by a stare at his watch from Simon didn't faze me. Was it talking to someone about my problems, or Jason himself, that improved my mood? He was certainly a good listener, but would I have felt the same talking to anyone with a sympathetic ear?

The day dragged by, and when I got home, I FaceTimed Beverley. She was always good company and I needed someone to chat and laugh with.

"What's up?" Bev always got to the point.

"Nothing special. Why should anything be up, just because I want to see my favourite sister?"

"Okay, okay, you want something from me; what time and where?"

Fifteen minutes later my sister appeared at my door.

Despite, or perhaps because of, our difficult early years, we were incredibly close. We didn't live in each other's pockets, but we were always there for each other when needed. We also invariably knew what each other was thinking, so, after asking about her latest art project, Beverley smiled sweetly at me. "Cut the crap, Paula, what's on your mind?"

Good question, I thought, what was on my mind? "You remember Brendan?"

"Do I remember Brendan? That tosser isn't back on the scene, is he?"

"No, he's not. As you know, he wanted me to move in with him and I wasn't ready to commit."

"Just as well."

"Okay, okay, it turns out he was seeing someone else at the same time."

"Seeing? He was sleeping with Angela Whore, for goodness' sake."

"That's very restrained coming from you Bev, and it was Moore, not Whore, I keep telling you."

"All right. He was shagging the ass off her. Is that better?"

"That's more like you."

"Look, where's this leading to, Paula?"

"I'm not sure. I'm just rambling, I guess. It's just that, at the time it knocked me sideways. Sort of put me off going out with men."

"Twelve months by my reckoning."

"Yes, well. I bumped into someone the other day and I found it refreshing, different, to just talk and have someone listen. Non-judgemental, being supportive."

Bev was suddenly serious. Gone was the bright smile and wide eyes. The vivacious, fun attitude was sidelined. Only those who were close to her knew that her appearance hid a sharp, intelligent mind. "You know what that means?"

"No, that's what I want to know."

"You're ready to go dating and share someone's bed again."

"Beverley!"

"What's he like? Has he got big feet? Do I know him?"

I sighed. "I haven't noticed his feet. I don't know what he's like, or whether I want to go on a date with him. What was the other question?"

"Do I know him?"

"No. He's the chap who drove into the back of me. I bumped into him again… Sorry, bad choice of words, that. I met him again by chance, that's all – nothing more than that."

"I see. Paula, after twelve months you're due for some serious attention, if you know what I mean?"

"I know exactly what you mean, you slut."

Beverley grew serious. "Paula, you are due to meet someone who really cares for you. Never settle for second best, or third best, like that tosser Brendan. Anyway, I must be going or I'll be late for my date."

"Of course you have a date, when haven't you?"

"Meow," she giggled, before bending and kissing me on the cheek, and made to leave. Then she hesitated and turned back. "Two things, Sis."

"What now?"

"Next time you see him, look at his feet."

I grinned. "And the second thing?"

"Make sure you do the driving."

Chapter 6

Matt

When Paula told me about the events at work, how badly and unfairly Simon Roach was treating her, my thoughts immediately went to the Davieses. It had been twelve years since our last dealings with them, but they were never far from my mind. History could never be ignored, especially when it concerned those evil people.

They first came on the scene when Emily moved to Bridgwater for her first job, teaching. A mugger had made off with her bag and Gordon Davies had come to her rescue. She often tried to rationalise and excuse the mistakes she made by blaming them on a feeling of loneliness and isolation. And, she claimed, there were certain similarities in Gordon's appearance to that of her long-lost best friend – me.

At first, he was attentive and thoughtful and she was sucked in. Too late, after he had more or less insisted that she move in with him, she realised that these qualities masked a serious need for him to control their life together. He even manipulated Emily into accepting his marriage proposal. Things came to a head in a curious fashion, and led to the ongoing hatred between the whole Davies family, Emily, me, and anyone connected to us.

It happened this way. Emily and I were best friends at primary school and when Emily's parents split she feared she would be moved away from Worcester, and we would be separated. We made a pact that if that happened, we would meet up in fifteen years' time in Weston. Why Weston? That's another story. Her words to me at that time, aged eleven, will stay with me for ever. "The only reason not to turn up is if you are dead."

I ummed and ahhed, before deciding to travel to Weston, prepared to be disappointed, which I was. She wasn't there. It was only by chance that I found out she had been involved in a car accident on her way to meet up with me. That was the first time I met Gordon Davies and my impression proved to be accurate. He was a control freak, a bully, someone so used to getting his own way. We nearly came to blows at Emily's bedside. It was then that she saw what her 'fiancé' really was. She handed her ring back, and finished with him, before moving to Malvern. But things really kicked off when I discovered that he had been embezzling Michael Davies Motors Ltd, his father's company, for some time. He lost everything: his job, house, car and his reputation. In desperation he turned up at Emily's house as somewhere to stay, regardless of what she wanted. The fight that ensued when I turned up by chance so nearly saw the end of me. Fortunately, the undetected use of my new mobile phone gadget, brought the police to my rescue in the nick of time, and saved me from being strangled. I was so close to meeting my maker. Gordon Davies was sentenced to ten years inside. The final glare and threats he made when he was led away stayed with me for many sleepless nights.

It was when Gordon's application for parole was rejected that his father sought retribution for his son with a number of devious and outrageous plots. The first entailed threatening one of his employees with the sack if his son didn't comply with his wishes. The young lad was in Emily's class at school. What Michael Davies demanded was that he cause such disturbance and mayhem that Emily would be forced to leave or, even better, be sacked. Fortunately, the father was a decent man and the plot was foiled.

Then came another plan that I so nearly fell victim to. It involved a gorgeous blonde called Judy Sayers. Emily was teaching in Bridgwater at the time, having moved away from me as she struggled to come to terms with her second miscarriage and the likelihood of never being able to conceive. Judy was enticed or threatened to seduce me then pretend to be pregnant. It was such an evil scheme.

It was later that night after Paula had left that I woke in the early hours and tossed and turned, unable to get back to sleep. My head was full of Emily and my history with the Davieses.

"You're very restless," said Emily, breaking into my thoughts.

"You can't sleep either?"

"Not with you constantly pulling the duvet off me." She relented and snuggled up to me. "You're worried about Paula and this Simon Roach, aren't you?"

"Yes, I can't help it."

"Do you think there's a connection?"

"What do you mean?"

"You know exactly what I mean, Matt. Whenever there's anything untoward going on, you're worried the Davieses are back on the scene lurking in the background. You think Roach may have some sort of ties to that lot."

I sighed and turned the bedside lamp on. "You're right, of course, I'm scared stiff they've returned to cause more pain. I need to find out more about Roach and his background. I've still got one or two contacts in Bridgwater from my couple of months working there while you were finishing your teaching with Molly Parker. If he does have any association with that place and that evil lot, I'll see what I can find out about him. Who he married, where he worked and probably, most important, who his friends are."

I felt Emily's hand caress my thigh. "I'll email my old teacher friend, Liz Potter. Just a sort of, 'not been in contact for a long time, how are you' type of thing. Find out if she's still with that monster Gordon, if nothing else."

"Good idea. I think I might sleep easier now." I didn't, of course. Try as I might, my thoughts kept returning to that day that would haunt Emily and me for ever.

It involved two characters who had befriended Emily at the writers' group that she frequented. It was only later, when it was too late, that we discovered they were anything but friends.

Chapter 7

Paula

I gradually got used to my somewhat restricted role at work. Having said that, I still resented being asked to do menial tasks that I felt I had outgrown, and hearing Simon on the phone to what should have been one of my clients. Then I seethed with anger for hours before normality returned.

What was strange was the changed attitude of the other members of staff towards me. When Colin Walker was there, I felt honoured if I got a good morning from any of them. I barely knew any of their names at that point and some I might not recognise outside of work, when they definitely would not have acknowledged me. Now, I got smiles. I heard tales of what they'd been up to the previous evening. They talked to me as if I were their friend, about anything but work. I sensed a sort of sympathetic hand being extended to me. I was now one of them. So much so, that one Thursday afternoon, Margaret Schultz asked me if I wanted to join her and a few of the others for a drink after work. This was a first. I felt it would definitely be the wrong move to turn it down, so I went along.

It was when we were huddled together at the bar in The Fox that Margaret turned to one of the others. Deborah, I think it was. "Can you see him? I can't." Deborah shook her head. "He'll probably be in later. It's still early yet."

I looked at them both, feeling lost in this conversation. I waited, wanting to learn more and to be part of this 'in' crowd.

Margaret looked at me, before explaining. "Someone I was chatting to last week. Said he knew you."

"Really?"

Just then the door opened and a small group of smartly dressed office workers entered. They moved urgently towards the bar. Margaret's eyes lit up as she spotted them.

"Hi," she shouted as she moved across to join them and immediately started talking to a good-looking man. Who was he? I didn't recognise him; he certainly didn't ring any bells. I stared across the room and watched him as he listened to Margaret's animated chatter. He became conscious of eyes focused on him and looked across to meet my gaze. I blushed as he smiled at me and turned away. How did he know me? He didn't mean anything to me.

"Deborah, who is…?" But she had turned away and was talking to someone from another work group. It wasn't long before I was left on my own and I made an uncertain beeline for the door. So much for a night out with friends. Margaret's man looked over to me, smiled and waved as I left.

The following morning I was sitting at my desk, trying and failing to muster up the motivation to tackle my inbox that seemed to be glaring at me, when Margaret arrived about ten minutes late. She looked hungover and although she tried to adopt her usual offhand manner, she was clearly on edge.

"You're a dark horse, aren't you?"

I looked at her in confusion. "Why, what d'you mean?"

She gazed across to where Deborah was sitting. "She likes playing the innocent," she spat out.

"I don't know what you mean. What am I supposed to have done?"

"You don't remember making eyes at George in The Fox last night?"

"I didn't; I just want to know how he…"

"Leave him alone – he's mine." Margaret shot me an intimidating glare and there was no hiding the menace that lay there.

"Of course." I stared down at the papers on my desk as she flounced off to her desk.

The following week followed the usual pattern, but by now I managed a fixed smile when Roach handed work out to me, and the other girls continued to be supportive. Having said that, I noticed that Margaret didn't invite me to the pub on Thursday.

It was on the Monday that I asked Deborah how the after-work drinks had gone. She looked slightly awkward and quickly cast her gaze around before answering, "Fine – Thingy was there this time."

"Who?"

"What's his name? I don't know his name. The one that Margaret is besotted with."

"But I thought she liked the one I saw last week, George."

"Oh, she likes him all right, but Thingy, she thinks is the real deal. She wants him for keeps and woe betide anyone who gets in her way." She gave me a hard, warning stare.

"But she's got nothing to worry about with me."

There was something of a sneer in Deborah's response. "Oh, come on. You must know how good-looking you are?"

"I don't know what you mean. I haven't been out with anyone for over twelve months. Since my boyfriend at that time cheated on me. Or had been cheating on me for some time."

Deborah relented, but only slightly. "Just don't get in Margaret's way, otherwise you'll regret it."

Chapter 8

Jason

I tried to find innocent ways to accidently bump into Paula, but to no avail. It was no good, I just had to bite the bullet and ring her. If she said no, then I would resort to plan C, whatever that was.

I rang her.

"Oh, it's you." Not encouraging.

"I just wondered if things were getting any better at work?"

"No. If anything, they're getting worse. Some of the girls aren't talking to me now and I haven't done anything."

"D'you want to talk about it? Not over the phone I mean, perhaps meet up somewhere?"

There was a pause. I crossed my fingers. "Okay."

We made arrangements for later that evening and I hurried off to get changed. But before I did, I dialled a number. It rang and rang, and just as I was about to give up, a voice came on the line.

"Hello?"

"I've got a date."

"You have? Well done. Just make the most of it."

I hung up and hurried off.

"Hi, Paula, what can I get you?" I noticed straight away that the smile she displayed did not come easily. She looked tired and unhappy.

I went to the bar and placed the two drinks on the table. "So work hasn't got any better, then?"

"No, only worse." I saw her studying me. "Tell me something about yourself. You know all about my problems, but I know nothing about you. Where d'you come from? How come you're loitering around the streets when you should be at work? What d'you do anyway?"

I held up my hand. "Wow. Let me answer one question before you fire another at me."

This time the smile was genuine. "Okay."

"Where do I come from? I guess 'under a mulberry bush' isn't acceptable?" I watched her lips curl downwards. "All right, I started life in Bromsgrove, Worcestershire and stayed there until I was sixteen. Then we moved down south, for three years, before moving back to the Midlands. What was the next question? Why wasn't I at work the other day? I can answer questions two and three at the same time. I've moved here for work, but I don't start until Monday, so I thought I'd have a good look around first. Get to know the place."

"That's sensible. You could practise your driving as well." She paused, then smiled to show there was no malice in the comment. "What do you do anyway, workwise?"

"I design websites."

Chapter 9

Emily

As I suggested to Matt, I emailed Liz Potter, just telling her what was happening in my life, and asking how things were going with her. We had not had any contact for many years, in fact since I had invited her to Harry's christening. Matt and I had thought long and hard before tendering the invite. What if she brought her husband, Gordon Davies? How would we react? Thankfully, she had written back, saying that they already had plans for that day, which couldn't be changed. Liz was a lovely lady, a fellow teacher at St Michael's, who though we had not been that close, so nearly had a profound and devastating effect on my life. Davies had used his charm on her to elicit my new address and he turned up on my doorstep. My mind shuts down when I think about what so nearly happened to Matt. It was about a week later that I received her reply.

> *Dear Emily,*
>
> *What a lovely surprise to hear from you! I still recall our time together at St Michael's with great affection. I wonder how our dear mentor Molly Parker is doing. Do you ever hear from her?*
>
> *Delighted to learn that Paula and Beverley are doing so well in their careers. Paula, a financial advisor – wow, that sounds so grand, so important.*

As for Beverley, making a living out of doing something she loves so much must be so satisfying. But Harry, he must be a dream come true for you and Matt. I'm delighted he's doing so well at school.

You asked how life is with me and Gordon. As you know it was always our intention to start a new life and put the past behind us. I would like to think that we have managed that. Gordon loves our quiet life and I know the people here adore him. He spends much of his time in the church choir, and running a local football team. And me? I spend most of my time by his side.

Then twelve months ago things changed. Gordon started to lose his balance when walking. He ignored this, as is his way, and then tremors started. We went to the doctor and after many tests they confirmed it. He has Parkinson's.

Gordon was very philosophical. He said it was God's punishment for him being such an evil person in his first life. It was what he deserved, he said, when he heard the diagnosis. That ignores the fact that now he is a wonderful, loving and caring person.

We are still incredibly happy. I cannot believe how lucky I was to meet Gordon. I pray to God every day, and thank him for my good fortune. With his help we will fight this disease together.

We must get together, perhaps a St Michael's reunion. Wouldn't that be fun?

Love,
Liz

I shut the email, feeling both happy and sad for Liz. Happy that her life had clearly been filled with love, for both Gordon and God. But sad that Gordon had been stricken with such a devastating illness. Then an image that I'd desperately tried to erase from my memory bank resurfaced. It was of Gordon Davies with his hands around Matt's throat as he sat astride him. It was the way his face was contorted with the effort of squeezing the life out his helpless victim that I could not shake off. I stood up with a cry of pain. That evil monster was right. The illness was punishment from above for the despicable, evil acts he'd heartlessly committed all those years ago.

It took a long time for my heart to stop racing and my pulse to return to normal.

When Matt returned later that afternoon, after visiting a client, I wordlessly showed him the email.

He looked over after he had finished reading, his expression thoughtful. "It's hard to believe that he's involved in anything sinister, with Roach or anyone. He probably has other things on his mind. Besides, from what Liz says, his focus is doing God's work rather than cooking up some devious plot against Paula."

"I think you're right. What about Tracy and Dan? Perhaps they're involved somehow."

"I could give Kevin, your old writing group friend a ring, assuming he's still on his old number. It's a few years since we last talked."

I nodded, my gaze returning to the email still open on my PC. My mind was in turmoil, the last twelve happy, contented years suddenly disappearing as the names, Gordon, Tracy, Dan and Kevin filled my head.

Chapter 10

Paula

"You design websites? That's cool."

A frown crossed Jason's face. "Well, that's what I really want to do. It's what I'm good at. But for now, I'm starting a new job tomorrow as I said, in IT. It's a nothing sort of job, but it will keep me going until I can start my own company. Anyway, that could be a long way off, and at present I'm a nobody, certainly nothing like as important as a financial advisor."

"If only," I sighed. "I've got used to Roach treating me like dirt, but now the girls have more or less sent me to Coventry."

"That's nasty. What have you done?"

"Nothing. That's the problem. One girl just doesn't trust me, and for no reason."

"Women!"

"Watch it. Then again, perhaps you're right. Why did you leave the Midlands in the first place?" I was keen to change the subject.

Jason's face took on a serious, faraway look. "My mother thought I needed a change. Well, I did need a change, to be honest. I got mixed up with the wrong crowd and was going in the wrong direction. She thought I needed a new start, and she was right."

"What direction were you going in?"

There was a hesitation. "A bad direction, that's for sure." He looked into my eyes for the first time since the question had been raised. "Okay, I'll level with you. I hung out with a gang that drank, did dope, did joyriding as a favourite hobby, and thought nothing of shoplifting just for the fun of it."

My mouth dropped open as I tried but failed to keep the horror from showing in my expression.

"There was no violence or anything like that," he said quickly. "But that was a long time ago. I'm not that person any more. I've been saved."

Jason must have seen the uncertainty in my face. "Look, this is not something I often talk about, but my dad died when I was twelve and I sort of lost my way. I was all over the place."

"It must have been difficult for you." This I could relate to.

"It was. Moving away was the best thing that ever happened to me. Until I bumped into you, that is."

"And bump into me you certainly did," I laughed.

He returned the laugh with interest. "That's not how I meant it, Paula."

"Until you bumped into me. That is just so naff, Jason Brown – you should be ashamed of yourself." But even as I spoke these words, I knew that my heart warmed at his unashamed pouring out of his past. He was not bad looking either, a gentle engaging smile with a well-toned physique. Stop it, I told myself. I've been around Bev too much; besides what did I really know about him? He could be another Brendan for all I knew.

Chapter 11

Jason

One minute she was laughing and gazing warmly at me, then it was as though the shutters had come down.

"So, moving solved everything, did it?" There was no attempt to hide the note of scepticism in Paula's voice.

"Yes – well not at first, but later, yes." I could see that she was still unconvinced. "Look, when we first moved, I was lonely, so I continued my bad old ways – ecstasy, cider, anything to dull the senses. Stop me feeling. And I did whatever I needed to do to get money to buy the stuff."

"I see."

"I never hurt anyone, physically that is – honestly, Paula."

"So why are you telling me all this stuff? You don't have to."

I reached over and took her hand. "That's an easy one. I want to get to know you better. I want you to know the good, the bad and the ugly side of me. I want more than the odd casual date with you."

She looked away, embarrassed, then turned back and stared straight into my eyes. "You're not married are you, or in a long-term relationship?"

"No," I chuckled, "cross my heart and all that."

"And you're not one of those guys who likes to have more than one girlfriend at the same time?"

The message became clear to me. "You've had a bad

experience, haven't you?" She didn't answer, but studied her fingernails instead.

"Paula, listen to me. I don't want lots of girls – I just want one girl who's special to me."

Chapter 12

Paula

I went to work the following day on a high. Jason was serious about me. "I just want one girl who's special to me," he'd said. After 'tosser' Brendan, Roach, Margaret and the other girls it's what I needed. All right, I wasn't sure of my feelings for him – it was too soon, but the boost to my morale was the important thing. Then came the call that shattered my illusion of happiness.

"Paula, step into my office, please."

I settled into the chair apposite my boss, my euphoria clouding any concerns I might have about what he was about to say. I should have guessed something was up; he rarely ever spoke to me, let alone called me into his office. I cursed myself later for not being more aware.

"Paula, you are no doubt aware that we opened an office in Bromsgrove last week?"

I nodded, thinking, What does that have to do with me?

"I would like to transfer you there, to give them some valued support." He fixed me with his small furtive eyes.

I was still not functioning properly. "For a week, two weeks? How long for?"

"They need proper support. I don't have any set time period in mind."

I slumped back in my chair in shock. All had become clear. "You're getting rid of me, aren't you? Booting me out. This is just the start." My voice got louder. "You've never liked me, have you, from day one?"

Roach raised his hand to silence me. "Your contract of employment is still with us. You're still a valued member…"

"Bollocks!" I shouted, before standing up and storming out of the office and out of the building.

"Colin."

"Hello?"

"Colin. I need to speak to you."

"Paula?"

"Colin, I hope you don't mind me bothering you, but I need to talk to someone. I've had a shit day." I knew I was on the verge of breaking down and struggled to rein it in.

"But Paula, I can't help. I don't work there any more."

"Who is it, dear?" I heard an old, distressed voice in the background.

I heard a muffled, "I'll be with you in a minute, dear."

"Colin, Roach has been awful to me from day one. Now he's trying to get rid of me. I don't know what I've done wrong." Despite myself, I felt a sob break free.

I heard the sigh down the phone. "There's something you need to know. I should have told you a long, long, time ago."

"Yes?" I urged. "Tell me."

"Colin, we have to leave now, this minute or we'll be late for your appointment." The voice was no longer in the background and was urgent and close to anger.

"Sorry, Paula, I have to go. Appointment at the hospital – can't be late."

"What's wrong?" I asked automatically without engaging my brain.

"Oh, it's chemo. Look, we will speak again soon. Just do as Roach says."

I was still clutching the phone as I tried to rationalise what Colin had just told me. Poor Colin had cancer. He hadn't left to spend more time at home, with his feet up. He'd left to deal with that evil disease. All of a sudden, my problems seemed trivial.

It was a quiet, uneventful evening. I did briefly toy with the idea of phoning Bev, but then decided against it. Turning to my younger sister for support whenever I had a problem just didn't seem right. Instead, I drew comfort from a bottle of red wine, which I nearly emptied, before retiring to bed. My head was swimming, both from the effect of the alcohol and the events of the day.

I twisted and turned as I reflected on how I had gone to work still savouring the heart-warming words of Jason, before being speared by Simon Roach's brutal tongue. But I did eventually come to a decision.

"Is Simon free?" I asked his secretary. It was clear from the way she avoided making eye contact that she was aware of how yesterday's meeting had unfolded. Besides, my slamming of the door as I stormed out of his office did not suggest a convivial discussion.

"Mr Roach can see you in five minutes, if you would care to take a seat."

I sat and waited – and waited. Colin had told me to trust Roach, and that was why I was here. As I sat, my mind circled backwards and forwards as it had last night. What was it that Colin should have told me a long time ago? It must have been important or he wouldn't have mentioned it. Had Uncle Matt called in a favour to get me my job? Yes – that was it! He had bribed, cajoled, or somehow made Colin take me on. Now that he'd left, that agreement no longer applied. Of course, it was so simple!

"Mr Roach can see you now."

I walked nervously into the office I knew so well. Roach held out his hand, indicating that I should sit. I sat. He said nothing, waiting for me to speak.

"I've come to apologise for how I behaved yesterday," I mumbled. "The news of my transfer came as a bit of a shock and I didn't deal with it very well."

He clasped his hands on the desk in front of him and nodded.

"I would like to go ahead with what you suggested," I continued. "I'm sure it will be good experience and benefit me and the company."

He sighed and stared right through me. "It will be good for your career – you need this. Trust me. I will give Brian James a ring and tell him you'll be there tomorrow morning to discuss your job role."

I felt confused.

Roach explained, "Brian James is your new boss. Any questions?"

I shook my head.

"You can take today off and make sure you are in the right frame of mind for tomorrow. We don't want any more misunderstandings, do we?" He picked up a file that lay in front of him and commenced reading. The meeting was over.

As I left his office, I was conscious of his secretary averting her eyes and studiously looking down at papers in front of her. The usually noisy office was deathly quiet, everyone absorbed in what they were doing as I collected bits and pieces from my desk. Only Deborah turned to me and offered an apologetic, sad smile. The hurt was too much. As I reached the door to leave the building I turned around. "I HOPE YOU MISS ME AS…AS… MUCH AS I'LL MISS YOU," I shouted.

I drove home feeling lost and lonely. After failing to distract myself with hoovering, washing and ironing, I wandered around the shops in town. I ended up buying clothes I didn't want, under the pretext of needing them for my 'interview' tomorrow. Then, when I returned home, I whiled away the hours until I could no longer look at my watch. Finally, I picked up my phone.

"Hi Jason," I said. "Just wondered how your first day had gone?"

"Oh, hi, Paula. It's good of you to call and check. Um – d'you want to meet up later and we can talk about it?"

Chapter 13

Jason

She sat opposite me, her brown eyes looking glazed and uncertain. "D'you want to talk about it?" I asked.

She fiddled with her drink. "Talk about what? I thought you were going to tell me about your day?"

I watched her fidget in her chair. Where had the confident, assured girl that I had first bumped into disappeared to? "My day was very much as expected. I met lots of very pleasant people, whose names and responsibilities I won't remember. But my job seems straightforward. I know I shall be bored with it in next to no time. Now, about your day?"

"That was a very brief résumé."

I spoke without thinking. "It's just a job. It's not important." I saw her flinch backwards in her chair as though she had been struck. "I didn't mean…"

"I know exactly what you meant. You think I'm overreacting. That what's going on at work – I've got out of all proportion. That's what you think, isn't it?" She spoke with anger, but even through the rage I could see vulnerability. I reached out to take her hand but she snatched it away. "You don't understand, do you? Ever since 'tosser Brendan' messed me about I've thrown everything into work. That's why what's going on now is so important to me."

"Paula, I know how—"

"I've taken work home most weekends. I've been on

45

investment courses, paid for by myself, and I've alienated myself from the others and put up with their sniping."

I tried to speak but she ignored me and continued. "Besides, it's in my genes. I need to have a goal, a reason to get up every morning. My mum…" She wasn't talking to me any more, but to an inner voice. "She would understand." She was gazing past me as if I wasn't there. "I have to go."

"Paula. Wait!"

But she stood up and left, without looking back.

Chapter 14

Paula

I had to know. I had to talk to Matt. It was unusual for me to simply turn up, without ringing first, but I had to know.

It was Matt who answered the door.

"Paula, what a lovely surprise." He threw his arms around me. "Emily, Harry!" he shouted. "It's Paula."

The usual love and tenderness that was always there engulfed me, making it impossible to bring up the subject that I was desperate to know the answer to. Particularly as Harry was sitting next to me, eager to talk.

"Harry, why don't you go upstairs and finish your homework?" suggested Emily.

"Mum?" he pleaded.

"You can talk to Paula later. And give her a thrashing at Plants vs Zombies, yet again."

He hurried off with a big grin on his face. "Of course I will."

"Now," said Matt, "what is it you wanted to talk about?"

I felt embarrassed about asking a question that I had posed to him before I first started work. It was as if I was questioning his honesty. But I had to go for it, as it was as if the whole thing was festering in my brain.

"You remember when I first went for my interview with Colin Walker?" I asked.

"Who?"

"Walker Investments. My employer."

"Oh yes. I remember." The confused look had gone.

I took a deep breath. "I know I asked you at the time and you said 'no' but – but the only logical reason I can see for how everything has changed, is if you got me the job in the first place."

"But Paula – I told you I didn't."

"Let me finish. As I see it, if Colin did some sort of deal, now that he's left, that deal no longer exists. So that's why Roach is free to do whatever he wants with me." I looked away, avoiding Matt's eyes. "You have to forgive me. The whole sorry chapter is getting me down."

Emily placed the cups of tea in front of us.

Matt said firmly, "Paula, please, this is exactly what happened. John Tate at Edwards Little, where I was working at the time, happened to mention that Walker Investments were doing really well. John looked after their accounts, you see, and Colin Walker had confided to him that he was looking to recruit. I gave Walker a ring to find out what he was after, what sort of person he wanted. Although he said he wanted someone with experience, I told him I had just the person for him." He smiled. "I convinced him that he might be able to save the expense and hassle of advertising, and that was the selling point. That," he said firmly, "is as far as my influence went, I promise you. No more than that."

"So, what did Colin mean when he said that there was something he should have told me about a long time ago?" I mused.

"Sorry, I didn't catch that. What did you say?" asked Matt.

"Nothing. I'm just talking to myself." I reached out. "I'm sorry, Matt. It's not that I don't believe you, it's just that I'm so confused. One minute everything is going perfectly, then the next – anything but. There has to be a reason."

Then Emily spoke. "I think you should tell her what you think, Matt," she said hesitantly.

I swivelled round to stare at her. "Tell me what?"

"What might, only might, be what's behind it all. It's only a thought. We have no proof," said Emily.

"It's what we always think, when something untoward or different happens," joined in Matt.

I felt alarm bells ringing as I cautiously asked the question: "What? What is it?"

"The Davieses."

I felt as though someone had punched me in the stomach. My voice when I spoke was raspy and choked. "Why are you telling me this, when you have nothing to say it's them?"

"Love, I know, there's nothing concrete. Emily has written to her old teaching friend Liz Potter and we know Gordon Davies is not involved. I'm still waiting to hear from Kevin, who I hope will give me some info on Dan and Tracy. It might not be them but, what I'm trying to say is, keep a sharp lookout. Be aware, be on your mettle, just in case." Matt looked across to Emily.

Emily explained: "What Matt is saying is that where the Davieses are concerned, it's better to be safe than sorry."

"But if it is them, what are they trying to achieve by ruining my career?" I knew tears were close to the surface and did my best to hold them back.

It was Emily who answered gently. "Their only aim is to cause pain, heartache and as much – how can I put it? – suffering, as possible."

I left with a heavy heart.

Chapter 15

Paula

I struggled for sleep that night as the Davieses swam round and round in my head. Despite that, when I met up with Brian James the following morning, I was determined to be at my businesslike best. I had to be positive. This was a new start, a new opportunity and to hell with my initial thoughts about being pushed out. My smart new clothes made me feel good about myself as I strode purposefully through the office doors.

"He's over there," said the well-dressed girl, who I took to be his secretary. I followed her finger to where a man not in the first flush of youth was crouched down, lifting a cup from a coffee machine. He turned around as he heard me, spilling the coffee as he did so.

"Damn," he said, studying the coffee that dripped down his trousers. "It's Paula Carter, isn't it?"

I held out my hand. "Pleased to meet you, Mr James."

He gave an awkward smile. "It's probably best if we don't…" He showed me his coffee-stained hand before leading me to the conference room.

He had grey hair and walked slowly, slightly crouching as if trying to protect his back. He sat down awkwardly on his chair. "Let me tell you a little bit about why this office came about and what the expectation is of this division."

I listened closely until there was a pause. "Thank you, Mr James, for giving me the background, but what is it you want me to do? Simon didn't explain that."

He smiled. "Please, call me Brian." I watched as he opened the folder in front of him. "You will work closely with me, as my assistant."

The confusion must have shown on my face. "What does…?"

But before I could finish, Brian interrupted. "Simon spoke very highly of you."

I was more confused than ever now. Roach saying something nice about me? It didn't seem possible.

"But he did say that you had certain things that you needed to address – to help with your career."

I sat up in alarm. "What things are those?"

Just then there was a knock on the door and four individuals strode in.

"Ah," said Brian, "let me introduce you to the rest of the gang."

My head was reeling as I shook hands with each of the staff and took in nothing of what was being said. It was clear that this was a regular morning meeting to review the day ahead. Then the girl who had first waved a finger in Brian James's direction appeared, pushing a trolley on which lay tea, coffee and biscuits. "Ah," said Brian with a smile, "another most important member of our team. This is Jane Moore." I instantly thought of Beverley's caustic comment on my ex's bit on the side, Angela Moore, who she always referred to as 'Angela Whore'. Then the voices became distant as my mind went into free fall. With the Davieses at the forefront of my thoughts, my battered and bruised senses returned to that dreadful day when 'whore' was used by that evil family to describe Aunt Emily.

"I'm sorry. I need the bathroom," I spluttered as I stood up. Brian looked at me in alarm.

"Are you all right, Paula?"

I nodded and moved away. It was only when I stepped outside the room that I realised that I didn't know where the bathroom was.

Chapter 16

Beverley

I drew up outside Paula's flat, noting her TT in the driveway. She was home, but then it would have been a surprise if she hadn't been. I pushed at the door to open it; it was locked. Paula never locked the front door when she was in. I pressed the doorbell and a few seconds later came the voice I knew so well. "Who is it?"

"It's your beloved sister. Are you going to let me in?"

"Oh, it's you."

I stepped inside and gazed at the worried frown. "'How lovely to see you!' or, 'It's my adored sister!' would have been better than, 'Oh, it's you'."

"Sorry, it's not been a good day." She disappeared into the kitchen then came back with a bottle of wine and two glasses.

I slumped down on the sofa. "I've just come from Uncle Matt's. He said you went to see him yesterday."

Paula studied me. "Did he tell you what he was worried about?"

I nodded. "The Davieses." It went quiet as we both considered this.

"Is that why you put a bolt on the door?"

It was Paula's turn to nod. It went quiet again. "Why was today so bad? D'you want to talk about it?"

She sighed. "I had this meeting with my new boss in the Bromsgrove office that I've been offloaded to. I wasn't really in the right frame of mind after my chat with Uncle Matt." She looked quizzically at me for my understanding. "My head was full of the Davieses. So, when one of the staff, Jane Moore, was introduced to me, I immediately thought of Brendan's whore, Angela Moore. From there it went to that dreadful day all those years ago."

I didn't need an explanation; I knew exactly which day she was referring to. I leaned into her. "Tell me about it. Tell me about that day. It's something that as a family, we never talk about. Look, I was only five at the time, too young to know what was going on. But I should know. If you are at risk, so am I. Sis, I need to know."

Paula lifted her glass and took a great gulp of wine before continuing. "You remember that day in the supermarket when I was abducted?" she asked.

"I knew something horrible happened, but what it was no one ever told me." I shrugged. "I was too young."

"I was never frightened for myself," she continued. "They never harmed or threatened me. But the things they talked about doing to Uncle Matt and Aunt Emily, particularly Emily, were grotesque. They referred to her as 'that whore', which is why my mind did cartwheels this morning. The language they used was obscene. Though I knew the words, to hear them used by adults with such hatred and venom was shattering."

"I know you were quiet and withdrawn for a long time afterwards, but I didn't know why – hardly surprising given my age."

"One of them said they should swap me for Emily and take it in turns with her. Then someone laughed and said it would be pointless as she would enjoy it. That laugh haunted me for years." She looked close to tears as she recounted the moment. "What I struggled to come to terms with for a long, long time, was the feeling of being as bad as them."

I stared at her. "What? How can you possibly say that?"

"Bev, you probably don't remember, but after we first came to live with Uncle Matt and Aunt Emily, I was dreadful to her – awful. I said some really nasty things, just to hurt her and all the time she was doing everything she could to make us feel loved and cared for."

"Sis, don't punish yourself. You were only eight and we had just lost Mum."

"I knew exactly what I was doing. You won't remember, but I do. One day I said to you, so Aunt Emily could hear, that after Dad died, Mum should have married Uncle Matt as she was still in love with him. But that was just one thing; I said so many other things."

"Is that why you never talk about that day?"

"No, it's not. It's because…"

"It's because you're still punishing yourself, isn't it? We trust each other enough to talk about anything, but that day has never been mentioned."

Paula slumped forward. "No, it's because I've shut it out from my mind. It never happened as far as I was concerned. That is, until Uncle Matt told me of his concerns about the Davieses last night."

I leaned forward and refilled her glass, aware of her anguish. "Sis, perhaps this Davieses thing is an illusion. Perhaps it's just…"

"I know, I know what you're thinking, and you may be right. You think that just because everything I've wanted to achieve has come my way, I'm a bit of a spoilt cow."

I tried to interrupt, but she continued. "You think that's why I can't cope with being pushed out from work. That it's a bitter pill that I can't swallow. It's not the job itself that's the problem, it's the sense of failure that I'm not used to. That's it, isn't it? I'm struggling to cope with it?"

"But you haven't failed. You've been moved."

"I know, but Colin, when I phoned him, said that there was

something he should have told me a long time ago, but before I could find out what it was, he had to go." Her voice went quiet. "He was off to the doctor. Poor Colin has cancer."

"Oh no." Just the word 'cancer' made me shudder.

Sadness filled Paula's face. "He told us he was stepping down so that he could spend more time at home, and put his feet up. That wasn't the reason at all."

A ringtone broke into the reflective mood that had filled the room. I made to move away as Paula dived into her pocket.

"Oh, hi Jason. No, you've no need to be sorry. It was me who was at fault. I was stupid."

Wow! Paula was apologising. I stared down at my feet, then clutched my hands across my heart before blowing a kiss. "See you later, Sis," I mouthed and let myself out.

As I drove home, my mind went over what Paula had said. All those years my confident, assured sister had pushed the trauma of 'that day' to a locked part of her brain that could not be entered. It was only when Uncle Matt had warned her of the Davieses' possible reappearance that the memories had resurfaced. How could she possibly consider herself bad because she had so wanted to remain loyal to Mum? Jason was exactly what she needed right now, for sure.

Chapter 17

Jason

It had taken me twenty-four hours to work up enough courage to ring Paula and apologise for my thoughtless comments. I thought I'd blown it. Imagine my surprise and delight when she said it was her fault. "I was stupid," were her words. I went for it. "Perhaps we should go out for dinner to sort out our misunderstanding?" It went quiet.

"All right, when did you have in mind?"

Wow, I hadn't expected that. "How about tomorrow, Cromwell's, I'll pick you up at 7.30?"

I waited.

"Okay."

Once we were out and had ordered food, we relaxed. "So, how's it going with your new job?" I asked.

She laughed, her chocolate-coloured eyes sparkling. "Today was okay, better than yesterday, that's for sure."

"That's got to be good. Why, what went wrong yesterday?"

"You don't want to know." She paused and thought. "Okay, I'll tell you. I had a meltdown when I was being introduced to my new work colleagues. To make it worse, I made an excuse that I had to go to the ladies, then when I stepped outside, I realised I didn't have a clue where I was going. I had to go back in the room and ask. How embarrassing was that?" She gave me a rueful grin. "Not a good start."

"You clearly got over it. You look back to your best this evening."

She took a sip of her wine. "That's down to Bev."

I gave her quizzical look.

"Bev's my sister. She has a way of putting everything in perspective and seeing the best in every situation."

"She sounds wonderful – almost as wonderful as her sister."

I watched her as she found it necessary to study the food that had just arrived. "So, d'you want to tell me what caused the meltdown?" I asked gently.

"Oh, a really bad day many years ago – you don't want to know about it." She took a bite of her prawn cocktail. "Um, this starter's delicious, what's yours like?"

I ignored her question as I thought about what she had said. "It must have been really bad if something that happened many years ago caused a reaction, or meltdown as you put it, yesterday?"

I thought she had chosen not to answer, as it went quiet. Then eventually in hushed tones: "It was to do with those evil Davieses, and I don't want to talk about it."

I couldn't help it despite her warning. "Davieses? Who are they?" My voice was a croak. I watched in alarm as the glass that was poised to her lips was slammed down on the table, spilling the contents. I could see tears at the sides of her eyelids as she stood up and snatched up her handbag.

"Please, I'm sorry. I didn't mean to upset you. Please." She sat hesitantly down. "Please stay," I said, indicating her food. She picked up her fork and slowly started eating. The relaxed appearance had disappeared and she looked pale and withdrawn. Conversation was awkward and stilted.

Later I drove her home, but before she got out of the car I reached over and took her hand. "Look, I'm really sorry I ruined the evening again. It was all my fault."

She gave me a wan smile. "It wasn't you; it was me."

"But I still don't understand."

She looked enquiringly at me.

I explained: "I don't understand how something that happened all those years ago caused such a reaction now?"

I watched her look away as she spoke. "It's Uncle Matt."

My face screwed up in confusion.

She continued, "He thinks the Davieses are back."

Chapter 18

Paula

Jason was concerned for me; that much was clear. The evening had been a write-off – no getting away from that. When I told him that Uncle Matt thought that the Davieses were back, his expression took on a look of shock and horror. It was odd. He phoned a week later, his tone guarded and conciliatory. "Could we get together and mend fences?"

We met up at The Fox and I greeted him with a warm smile to start the evening in the right way. I was determined that this time things would be better. Jason handed me my drink and we began a 'what have you been up to' conversation. Then a body in a low-cut dress and high, toppling heels stepped between us and a hand reached up and brought his mouth to hers in a hungry kiss.

"Hello, darling," she gushed, taking his hand. "Haven't seen you in here for a few weeks." I was stunned, watching as Jason tried to push her away, his face flushing.

"Margaret, no I've been busy. This is Paula. Paula this is…"

"Oh, Jason, there's no need for intros – we know each other very well, don't we?" Although she was smiling, there was no hiding the icy-cold hatred in her eyes as she spoke. "I didn't know you two knew each other, but then I should have guessed. There's not many good-looking men that Paula hasn't been with, if you know what I mean, is there, darling?"

My mouth flew open in shock. How could she?

"I hope I haven't spoken out of turn. But friends should be open with one another, shouldn't they, darling." Her eyes grew wide in feigned innocence.

I was just about to lay into her and demand that she apologise for her outrageous lies, when she continued.

"Walker Investments are doing really well now. Everyone is happy and working together as a really friendly team. The improvement over the last two weeks has been amazing, since, well, since the change of staff."

Once more I was gobsmacked. I saw Jason look pityingly at me.

"Anyway, I must leave. See you around, Jason. We must get together again." She gave him a long and lingering look, then gave me a contemptuous glare and sloped off, wiggling her bottom as she did so.

"Friend of yours?" asked Jason with an earnest expression.

"She's someone I used to work with. No – she's definitely not my... But what about you? Is she your friend or is she more than that?"

He held up his hand to stop me, before bursting into laughter. I looked at him in amazement before his infectious laugh made the anger disappear and I collapsed into uncontrollable laughter with him.

We had a relaxed, comfortable evening where we felt like we had known each other for years. It was when he drove me home and pulled up outside my flat that I felt I had to know; I had to ask him. "You didn't believe her, did you?"

"About what?"

"You know? About knowing lots of men." I was glad for the darkness so he couldn't see the red blush that was descending down my body. He leaned over and his lips met mine. When he broke away, my eyes were still closed.

"She was talking about herself, Paula, and before you ask,

no we didn't. When I first moved here I didn't know anyone, so I went to The Fox as it seemed a good place to meet people. As soon as I walked in, she pounced. I more or less had to fight her off. Look, I know who I want to be with and it isn't her."

I felt myself go hot and I opened the car door. As I leaned back in to say goodnight, his eyes fixed on mine as he spoke. "Don't worry, I'm not going anywhere."

Chapter 19

Paula

We became good friends, meeting up two or three times a week. Okay, Jason wanted to be more than just buddies – he had made that absolutely clear – but I wasn't ready, despite what Bev might say. I thought of it as the 'Brendan' factor. Whenever we came back from the theatre or cinema and he would say with a hopeful look, "I can stay if you want?", Brendan's cheating would flick through my mind and I would shake my head.

One Saturday morning I visited the supermarket, to buy some ingredients to make a spicy Indian dish for Jason and me. I joined the checkout queue and was busy unloading my goods onto the counter, when I looked up and gave a horrified gasp. The man in front of me was Simon Roach. Some instinct made him turn around and his expression became guarded as he saw me.

"Paula, how are you? Well, I hope?"

I nodded before risking my voice and croaked, "Fine, Simon. How are things at Walker Investments?"

"Very good, very good indeed. I'm often in contact with Brian James and he tells me you are coming along well. The move has worked well. He's very pleased with the progress you've made in certain areas…but this isn't the right place to talk about that." His wife passed a shopping bag to him.

"Which areas are those?" I tried, but it was no use – I was only talking to his back. I left the supermarket in turmoil. Just those few moments with his eyes boring into mine had shredded my confidence. What was it I needed to work on? It had been mentioned before, but I still didn't know what it was.

The special Indian cuisine was a disaster, my mind elsewhere. I was halfway through cooking when I remembered that Uncle Matt had said that he was going to find out more about Roach. Had he? He hadn't said anything to me. I phoned.

"Paula – how lovely to hear from you. How are things?" Uncle Matt always sounded relaxed and caring. He talked for several minutes, mostly about what Harry had been up to. I listened, growing more and more impatient until I finally interrupted.

"Uncle Matt, it's really important. I have to know."

"Yes, Paula, I'll help if I can. What is it?"

"Did you find anything out about Simon Roach?"

His tone was different when he answered. "No, I haven't, why what's happened?"

"Nothing's happened. It's just that I bumped into him in Sainsbury's and it bothered me. There's something about him. I don't know what it is, I can't put my finger on it, but he just unsettles me."

There was a pause before Uncle Matt answered. "A couple of old work contacts told me they knew of him, but there's nothing untoward. I'll try Kevin again, he knows everyone. I've left messages but he's not phoned back. I'll try him once more. In the meantime, try not to get too wound up."

My nose twitched as I became aware of the smell of burning. I turned to see smoke rising from the wok. "Oh, shit. Must go – my dinner's burning. Love you."

I scraped the burnt bits off my chicken tikka, but my nerves remained frazzled. When the doorbell rang minutes later, and I let Jason in, I was more than ready for the red wine that he handed me.

"Mm, the dinner smells delicious," he said, lying outrageously.

It was a pleasant evening, though I was content to let Jason do most of the talking. I did most of the drinking. Through the fog that was descending, my mind kept returning to Roach. We watched the old film he chose on Netflix – *Doctor Zhivago*. After the credits rolled, I felt his arms around me as he snuggled up on the sofa. "You didn't take any of that in – you were miles away. D'you want me to stay?"

I felt a warm glow; I was wanted. "That would be good."

We made love that night for the first time.

Chapter 20

Jason

"What a marvellous feeling it is to have a boyfriend I can trust again," she'd said as she snuggled up to me.

Later I phoned my friend and told him that things had moved on. I didn't go into details; it didn't seem right.

"Wonderful," he said. "I'm really happy for you."

We chatted for some time before hanging up. I could tell he was pleased for me, and it was only the start. Confirmation that I was 'in' with Paula came when I was invited round to her parents' house in celebration of her dad's birthday. I was as nervous as hell as we arrived at their door. Paula pressed the doorbell, then let us in.

"It's me," she announced.

I watched, my heart pounding as two figures came towards us. I saw straight away that Uncle Matt had a warm open face that glowed as he gave me a hearty shake of the hand. I offered him the bottle of wine I'd brought with me. "Happy Birthday, sir."

"It's Matt, Jason, and thanks for this – very thoughtful."

I turned towards Emily, unsure whether to kiss her cheek, but there was a more cautious, guarded look in her eyes. "Jason, how good to meet you at last."

Dammit – how stupid was I? Why hadn't I found out what flowers Emily loved, and bought the biggest bouquet I could? I would learn for next time, that's for sure. Harry wasn't a problem. As soon as Emily's scrummy dinner was over, I showed him things on his computer that made him gasp in delight; I was his friend for life. Matt couldn't have been more helpful. Paula had clearly briefed him on my plans to start my own website business and he had lots of sound advice that he offered me, together with a whole load of useful contacts.

I was in deep conversation with Harry when Paula appeared. "It's card time – Gin Rummy. There's no way out – family tradition."

We settled down and played the silly game with voices rising, the table being thumped and chairs being pushed back as 'unlucky' players took umbrage. Underneath this charade, the warm, loving family atmosphere filled the room with laughter bouncing off the walls. I felt comfortable and at home.

"It's a pity Beverley couldn't make it," Emily mentioned.

"One of those things. Building her career is important. She's an artist," Matt turned to me and explained with obvious pride.

I nodded. "Yes, a very good one. Paula told me."

Emily looked at Paula. "Have you seen the birthday card Bev left?"

I watched Matt pass it to Paula, who read it and handed it back. No words were spoken but the look they exchanged was full of emotion they couldn't suppress.

It was later that Paula told me what her sister had written on the card. "My birth mum and dad will always have a special place in my heart, but never a day goes by without me thanking God for bringing you and Aunt Emily into my life."

I looked at her, waiting for her to explain. Instead, she adopted an air of nonchalance. "Bit special, my sis." She kissed me. "My family all really took to you."

I smiled. "They were lovely, as I knew they would be."

I returned to my flat that evening as Paula had an early start the following morning. I lay in bed and let my thoughts drift. Had I ever been part of a loving, supportive household?

The answer to that was easy: never. Until, that is, I moved to Bridgwater, where it wasn't a family in the normal sense of the word but a community. That was the first time I experienced real affection and unequivocal support. It was so new to me that it was some time before I could accept it. Now the person who was the lynchpin of such a community, was a heart-breaking shadow of his former self.

Chapter 21

Paula

Over the course of the next few weeks, my life became more settled, with Jason playing an important part in that. I didn't scowl as much as I had done post-Brendan and we often settled down in the evening with a glass of wine, just talking. Okay, we usually found other things to do later, but it wasn't all about that. Our relationship became commonplace and routine in the best possible way. I could rely on him; he was supportive and loving.

One evening as I arrived home from work, my mobile started buzzing. It was Colin. If I didn't have anything else on, could I pop round later.

"Colin, what is it?" I was confused. "Can't you tell me over the phone?"

"Not really, it's some things I should have talked to you about a long time ago."

I was apprehensive when I pressed the doorbell and waited. When he answered the door, my hand flew to my mouth in shock. He kissed my cheek and gave me a gentle smile, as he tried to reassure me as he always had. He showed me into the lounge where he slumped down onto the sofa, clearly worn out from the exertion. What was left of his hair was white and his face was pale and gaunt. I should have asked how his chemo was going, how he was feeling, at least shown interest in his wellbeing. Instead I blurted out, "What did you want to tell me?" His eyes seemed to droop still further.

"You know what happened when your Uncle Matt contacted me?"

"I think so," I replied cautiously.

"Well, I only agreed to see you because it was Matt. I needed someone with experience, but he has a way of getting what he wants, does Matt. But when I met you it changed my life for ever."

I gave him a puzzled look. But as I was about to interrupt him with the obvious question, he held up his hand to stop me. "Let me explain. Nineteen years ago, Carol and I had a child: Jennifer Sarah. Jenny was our life." He paused as he disappeared into another world. "She was just eleven years old when she contracted neuroblastoma, a rare disease, and died. Just one child in 7,000 ever gets it, so the doctor informed me."

My heart sank as I took this in. "That's awful, Colin. I can't imagine how dreadful that must have been. But forgive me, what has that to do with me?"

His sad eyes fixed on mine. "When you stepped through the door into my room, I was hit by the way you walked. Then as we started talking, it was the way your hand went to your chin when you were thinking, your spontaneous laugh, the chocolate brown of your eyes. I was sent back in time. You were her – you were Jenny, brought back into my life."

"And that was why you took me on, because I reminded you of Jenny. That was the only reason?"

"Yes, Carol told me not to – but I didn't listen."

"Excuse me." I felt blood rush to my face as I stood up to leave, nearly tripping over my feet.

"Paula, wait – please, let me finish."

I sat back down, my heart pounding as his wife appeared with tea and biscuits. She looked at Colin with concern. "Remember, you promised you wouldn't get too wound up."

"I know, I know," he said with a weak smile.

"Good, I'll leave you then." She gave me a hard glare before shutting the door."

"So, I would not have got the job, but for my likeness…if I didn't remind you…?

Colin reached out and took my hand. "Listen – Matt was right, you were exceptional. Everything you were told you took on board. You listened and learnt and worked harder than anyone else at the company. I needed to tell you this. I had to be honest with you."

I was confused. "Thank you, Colin. But what is it that you, Simon Roach and Brian James keep telling me I need to work on? I need to know – it's driving me mad not knowing."

"Ah. It's not your fault, Paula, it really isn't – it's mine. Because I mentored you and pushed you on."

"Because I reminded you of your daughter," I interrupted.

His face clouded over. "Not just because of that. But the other staff saw it as favouritism, and it was clear that they would never work with you. That's why Simon moved you on. It was the right thing to do."

"So that I could learn to work with others? With people who don't know me?"

"That's right." He fixed me with a sorrowful gaze? "I needed to tell you this. I need to clear up loose ends before I…"

I jumped up. "Colin, don't say it – you're going to get better, I know it." I felt his frail arms encircle me.

"I've had a wonderful life and now – now it's time."

The following morning, I awoke feeling both sad and pleased. Sad because it was clear that my friend and mentor had few days left on this earth. Pleased because I was certain that I could easily deal with my shortcomings, but there was also something else. When it was a reasonable hour, I phoned home. It was Aunt Emily who answered.

"Paula, love, how good to hear from you."

We chatted, mostly about Harry, then she asked. "What's up, Paula? What's on your mind?"

"I just..." I hesitated. "Okay, there's something I need to tell you and Uncle Matt."

I heard the gasp. "You're not pregnant, are you?"

I laughed. "What a thing to suggest! No, I'm not pregnant."

"Thank God for that. It's too soon. We'll see you this evening then."

Chapter 22

Paula

I looked at the face before me and noticed the wrinkles around the eyes and the grey hair at the side of his head. If anything, they made him even more loveable. "I need to apologise, Uncle Matt."

"Oh, fair enough – accepted – what for?" His mouth lifted into that well-loved grin.

"I doubted you and shouldn't have."

Uncle Matt stared at me in confusion. "Paula, what are you talking about?"

So, I told him.

"Wow. I didn't even know Colin had a daughter, but then I only knew him through business – balance sheets and the like. I can't imagine losing a daughter so young. It must have been hell."

I watched as he considered what I had told him. "So, Simon Roach isn't the ogre you thought he was?"

"No," I agreed. "He still has an unsettling way of looking at you, well, me at least, but that's all. And that's why I wanted to see you."

He lifted his eyebrows as he stared at me. "Go on, explain."

"It means that the Davieses are not back on the scene, thank God."

He let out a sigh and slumped back in his chair. "Thank the Lord for that. All that worrying for nothing."

*

I returned home and settled down on the sofa with a book, though I found myself staring sightlessly at the same words for what seemed like hours. The image of my mentor's tired, doomed face filled the page. I kept seeing the gentle expression as he said, "I need to clear up loose ends before I…"

It took a few seconds before my ears and brain engaged together to hear the buzz of my phone. "Hello?"

"Paula, at last. I've been trying you all evening. Are you all right?" The concern in Jason's voice was evident.

I sighed. "It's been a difficult day, to say the least."

"As long as you're all right. When you didn't show at the Swan I thought you'd had an accident, or even worse, you'd ditched me."

I started to laugh, then the penny dropped and I took a sharp intake of breath. "Oh, Jason, what with what's been going on I completely forgot. I'm really sorry."

"That's okay, I understand. Shall I come round and you can make it up to me?" The request was accompanied by a gentle laugh.

Chapter 23

Jason

I was really worried when Paula failed to show. Had I done something wrong? Had someone said something to her about me? Then, when she eventually answered the phone, I found she'd forgotten me! Forgotten our date! But any annoyance soon disappeared as we talked. She sounded sad and distracted. I suggested going round to her, but she gently turned me down. "Not in the right frame of mind. Not good company." She promised to make up for it the following evening, when I turned up with an expensive bottle of Merlot.

She tried to explain. "You know I told you about my old boss Colin Walker who sort of mentored me when I first started at Walker Investments? He was as helpful and encouraging as Simon Roach is cold and nasty. Well, I went to see him the day before yesterday and almost didn't recognise him – he's dying." I watched as her eyes drooped down. "He has cancer."

I was just about to reply when a bright female voice burst forth from the hallway. "Hi'ee – it's your favourite sister. The door wasn't locked, so everything is tickety boo again?"

I stared at the girl who had just entered the room.

"Ooh, so sorry, I didn't mean to interrupt."

She was mesmerising. Slim with long blonde hair. But it was the radiant full-of-life expression that was captivating.

Her hands went to her chin in mock embarrassment. "Shall I go? Leave you to…?" Her gaze flitted from me to Paula. She slowly asked, "Is this who I think it is…?"

"Yes, this is Jason. Jason, this is my impossibly infuriating sister Beverley. Once met, never forgotten."

I laughed at the clear bond that existed between them.

"Jason," gushed Beverley. "Paula has not stopped drooling about you for weeks."

The merriment shone from her bright eyes as she looked at her sibling. It was impossible not to follow every movement of the blue orbs.

"Beverley! Will you stop it!" said Paula, hands on hips, as she glared at her sister.

"Okay, okay, that's a bit over the top. Should I just say that she's only mentioned you once or twice?"

Paula looked questioningly at her sister, knowing there was more to come.

"In every sentence, that is." She ducked as a cushion came flying towards her.

Things cooled down with the aid of a glass of wine. Then Beverley faced Paula and said, "I popped around to Uncle Matt and he told me about your old boss, Colin Walker. I know how much you respected him and thought you might be feeling low and could use a bit of support, but it looks like Jason had the same idea." She stood up and fixed those bright eyes on me. "It's good to meet you, but I know when two is company and three's a crowd. I'm sure we'll meet again."

"Beverley, you don't have to go on my account. You stay and talk to your sister," I insisted.

"Look," said Paula, "why don't we arrange a foursome? Go out for a meal one day next week? I'm sure Bev can seduce, sorry, encourage one of her many men friends to come along. What d'you say, Bev?"

"Um, I'm not sure. I'll need to check my diary – see if I have a free evening." She adopted a haughty tone as she raised her nose to the ceiling.

It seemed strangely quiet and flat after Beverley left. The sparkle that had found its way into Paula's face disappeared. "Come on," I said, taking her hand in mine. "Let's go for a wander."

We walked along the riverside, basking in the tranquillity that the gentle ripple of water offered, watching the many swans swimming along in their quiet, graceful manner. The cathedral peered over the river, adding its architectural splendour to the view. We paused to take a sip of water. Paula asked, "So, what did you think of my sister, then?"

Chapter 24

Paula

"Get that, will you?" shouted Beverly over the sound of the gushing shower water. "It's on the bedside table."

We had arranged a sibling night out, and as usual my sister was running late and I was left twiddling my thumbs while she got ready. But I did as I was asked as usual, and picked up the phone.

"Hi, Beverley."

"It's not Beverley – she's otherwise engaged. Who is this?"

The line went dead. I stood holding the phone to my ear, confused. I was still puzzling over the call when my stunning sister eventually appeared. "We're only going out for a pub meal, Bev, not an upmarket celebrity restaurant."

"I know, I know, I just threw some old stuff on. Who was that on the phone?"

"I've no idea. As soon as I said you were otherwise engaged, he hung up."

Beverley shrugged.

"It sounded just like Jason, but it can't have been! I must be going mad."

"What did he say?"

"He only asked for you." I looked at my watch. "Sis, we'd better hurry, we're already late. Can we talk about it later?"

Chapter 25

Jason

"So, what's she like – the other one – the sister?"

I was on the phone to my friend, updating him on what I'd been up to since the last time we spoke.

"Superb figure, long blonde hair, vivacious, full of life."

I heard the chuckle. "Sounds like she lured you in, no problem."

"It's impossible not to be entranced." A picture of the bright eyes and luscious lips flashed before me as I spoke.

"Um, I'll take your word for that."

"But she and Paula are very close, that much is obvious. They look out for one another. Something to do with a difficult early life."

"Really?" My friend laughed. "I think we know where to go from here then, don't we?"

"We do?" I queried.

So, I listened, instinctively nodding my head as he explained.

The next few days I gazed at my computer at work and my TV screen at home and registered nothing. It had all sounded so easy when I was talking to my friend Steve. Now I felt isolated and vulnerable. Could I really do what we had agreed? Could I really pull it off? In my darkest moment when doubts filled my head, I thought of how my life had been turned around after arriving in Bridgwater. Oblivion or prison for certain, had been staring me in the face, but instead I got my life back on track, against all odds. Tears filled my eyes when that kindly face appeared before me. I snatched up the phone. "Hi, Beverley."

"It's not Beverley – she's otherwise engaged. Who is this?"

I stabbed at the off button. Had she recognised my voice?

I met up with Paula the following day and I tried super hard to be relaxed. After the briefest of kisses, she said, "I met up with Beverley last night."

Oh no. This was it. Over before it had started.

She continued, "You remember we talked about getting together with Bev, and one of her men friends? Well, she has Trevor lined up for next Friday if that suits?"

I mumbled an, "Okay – that's great."

Chapter 26

Paula

We settled down in the country pub for a relaxing evening. I leaned back in my chair as Beverley's lively chatter took over. I was well used to it. It wasn't as if she wanted to hold forth, it was simply Beverley being Beverley. There had been many occasions when I had been more than grateful for my sister making a dreary evening acceptable, with her endless lively chatter.

"So, I opened this gate and went into the field, even though Mum and Dad had told us not to." She looked from Trevor to Jason, then to me before continuing. "Well, I tripped over the fence and my wonderful, caring sister dived over the gate to make sure I was all right. She landed in a huge pile of cow shit. Mum, when she saw what had happened, came racing over. She gave the brown stuff the more acceptable name of 'cow pat' before taking us home, but at a discreet distance. So, for the rest of the day Paula was called Pat."

Trevor and Jason laughed appreciatively though my attention wandered as I'd suffered the story many times. Then some second sense made me gaze over to my left, and there was a sight I hadn't ever wanted to see again. The dark hair and earnest expression I could never forget as he gazed into the eyes of the blonde sitting opposite. I quickly looked away.

"Shall we go onto The Red Lion?" I stood up, my back to the other table.

Beverley sat motionless, eyes wide in astonishment. "But we've only just got here."

"Please? The Red Lion's much better."

As we moved towards the exit, Beverley nudged me and whispered, "What was that all about?"

"Tell you later."

"What are you two plotting?" inquired Jason with a grin. "Trevor, we need to watch out for these two."

The rest of the evening was a blur. I desperately wanted to get involved in the conversation but felt out on the edge, an interloper to someone's private party.

"Super evening," smiled Trevor after the taxi dropped us off back at my flat.

"D'you want me to stay?" murmured Jason as his lips found mine.

I shook my head. "Too tired and stuff to do early tomorrow."

He kissed Beverley on the cheek. "Look after your sister." He rushed off to catch up with Trevor, no doubt to share their view on the evening.

"So, what happened, then?" Straight to the point was my sister.

There was no point in prevaricating, so I told her.

Bev uttered a loud sigh. "That tosser ruined your evening, yet again!"

"He was with Angela Moore."

"So, he's still shagging her, then. You're well rid of that toe rag. Well, aren't you?"

I nodded as Beverley brushed the hair out of her eyes and gave me a hard look. "You've got Jason now. You need to move on. What's wrong with you? Aren't you happy with him?"

"Off course I am. He's kind, supportive, always listens when I'm moaning."

"There's a but in there somewhere, I can sense it."

"No, there's no but."

It went quiet, which is unusual when Beverley is around. Finally, I had to ask: "What is it? What are you thinking?"

"It's you. I'm worried about you. There was me thinking that you had finally found happiness with someone who is considerate and thoughtful – your words. Only to find 'tosser Brendan' still has this strange hold over you, and he's exactly the opposite. What's going on with you?"

I shook my head and tried to appear at ease with myself. "Nothing's going on."

Beverley disappeared into the kitchen and came back with two cups of coffee. "There's something else, Sis." She placed one in front of me. "Does it not seem odd to you that you have not seen hide nor hair of Tosser since you split up last year? Then, as soon as you start going out with Jason and looking happy and settled, he makes an appearance."

Chapter 27

Matt

'Thwack.' I jumped up in alarm as the pen struck the newspaper.

"What's that for?"

Emily smiled across at me. "You're not asleep, I can see that, but you've been gazing at that same page for the last half an hour. That usually means that you are deep in thought about something, so what is it?"

I dropped the newspaper into my lap. "You don't miss a thing, do you?"

"I shouldn't, not after thirty-odd years. So, spill it – what are you worried about?"

"Worried is too strong a word. It's just that I tried to contact Kevin, to see if he knew anything about the Davieses, as you know. Well, I've still not heard from him."

Emily took my hand. "But I thought Paula reassured us that yours fears about that evil lot were unfounded."

"Yes, love, I know. But after casting my mind back to that time, it got me thinking – how good it would be to make contact and find out how things panned out for him and his sister."

"Stop worrying. I'll get in touch with the old writing group and see if I can get any info. Trust me."

Later, I listened as Emily phoned the leader of the writing group. It was while she was a member of that group many years ago that she first met Kevin, Dan and Tracy. She thought that the latter two were her friends. How wrong she was.

"Yes, that's right, about fifteen year ago," I heard her say. "I see. Could you give me the number of the previous group leader, then? No, I understand." I heard a tortuous sigh. "Could you ask him to ring me instead?"

It was the start of a long process. Then one evening the phone rang and I heard a voice that I hadn't heard for many a year, but which was instantly recognisable.

"Matt Bishop, how the devil are you?"

"Kevin, at long last! How good to hear from you. Emily and I have been trying to track you down for ages. Where are you living these days?"

"I'm in Paphos," answered Kevin.

"Cyprus. Are you on holiday? It must be a long one, that's for sure."

"No, I live here now. It's a long story."

"Tell me."

I heard a deep sigh. "Where to start. You know my sister went off the rails all those years ago after THAT party?"

I recalled the horrible story he had related to me that had left me stunned. His sister had been invited to a party organised by Dan Davies. At first it had seemed a friendly, social evening, but it turned into a horrific nightmare. Her drink had been drugged and when she came round, she found herself in bed with Davies. Laughingly, he told all his drunken so-called mates what an insatiable shag she was. It was many moons later that Kevin discovered that Davies's preferences were for men and that his so-called conquest with Julia never happened. It was merely an attempt to portray himself as a normal hot-bloodied male to his boozy friends.

I returned to the present. "Yes, I remember."

"Well, she was still in a dark place after you left Bridgwater. No longer on drugs, but deeply unsure of herself, and relationships were a no go. Then she met some chap who was caring and attentive. That was it, they were married two months later. But it was only six months after that that she found he was caring and attentive to lots of other women as well. She gave him the boot. Not surprisingly, she felt she needed to start a new life, and I decided to join her. That's when we moved to Cyprus – start afresh and all that. Leave the bad stuff behind."

"There was plenty of that, poor girl – she deserved happiness. Did it work?" I asked.

Kevin's chuckle took me back in time. "It certainly did. She passed her exams, then she found a proper person, the sort my sister deserves. She married again and has a daughter aged eight. A real darling is Katie. Julia's incredibly happy at long last."

"Brilliant, there is a God. And you – what about you?"

"I met someone. Things are good. Anyway, that's enough about us. I figured you've been trying to get in touch with me for a reason – and that reason is usually the Davieses."

I laughed. "The brain's still working, Kevin."

"Only just."

I cut to the chase. "Something untoward happened to Paula at work and my first reaction was the Davieses were back on the scene, but I've since learnt that I was wrong."

"Okay, that's good. If you want me to find out what they've been up to I can try my contacts back in Bridgwater for reassurance? The last I heard is that Dan took over ownership at Davies Motors, but before he did, he got married."

"He did?" I queried. "Who to?"

"He married Tracy."

"What? But I thought Dan was…"

"I know, I know. The thinking is that Michael Davies made it a condition of his will that Dan present an acceptable face to the public if he wanted ownership of the company. Michael Davies was very old-fashioned in his outlook."

We chatted for some time before Kevin rang off, promising to phone again if he found out anything else of interest.

Chapter 28

Paula

Was Beverley right? Though she always had many admirers, none of her relationships had ever come close to anything lasting. So, did her comments have any substance? Did Brendan still have some sort of hold over me? And deep down, what were my true feelings for Jason? Was I being unfair to him?

I felt confused, all these concerns swimming around in my head as I threw myself into work over the next few weeks. Brian was left desperately trying to keep me occupied. Whenever Jason rang, I put him off. I needed space and time to think. I kept asking myself whether the amount I missed him was enough. Was it my head or my heart that needed him?

One evening Jason rang and I put him off with a fictitious prior arrangement, feeling guilty after listening to his obvious concern about me. The following morning, I received a letter through the post. I picked up the envelope and immediately recognised the handwriting. My heart was pounding as I opened it. Jason had given up on me. Had he sent me an old-fashioned farewell letter? There I was trying to discover my true feelings for him and he had given me the boot. I gasped as I stared at the two tickets to see *Les Misérables* at the Birmingham Hippodrome tomorrow evening. How did he know the show was my favourite? There was no way I could refuse. I picked up my phone and hurried out a text.

The following evening, I watched from my bedroom as Jason strode cautiously down the drive. His hands were thrust into the pockets of his jeans and his head was down. His mouth was a straight line and his brow was furrowed.

As soon as I opened the door, he stepped back, his eyes wide in alarm as I flung my arms around him.

"Paula, wow. I think you're pleased to see me." His mouth creased into a big grin. "Thank goodness for that – I thought you'd had enough of me."

We settled down in the theatre and I sat entranced, listening to the emotion of the songs. When Fantine sang 'I Dreamed a Dream' I wondered: was Jason my dream? I knew Brendan was my distant, bad past. Whether Beverley was right, and he had intentionally reappeared on the scene, made no difference, he was nothing to me any more. Angela Whore was welcome to him! Jason was thoughtful, considerate and loving.

We returned to my place after the show, where after a couple of glasses of wine we moved to the bedroom. After making slow, gentle love I gazed up at him. "How did you know *Les Misérables* was my favourite?"

"Beverley told me."

"Huh, that figures. She knows everything about me. Never misses a thing, that girl."

Chapter 29

Beverley

I heard the doorbell ring and watched Paula's face as she entered.

"Hi, Sis. You okay?" I asked.

I retreated to the kitchen without waiting for an answer and put the kettle on.

"I'm fine – Jason and I went to the theatre last night. *Les Mis.* Brilliant. But then you knew all about it, didn't you? Interfering cow."

"Paula, I was only trying…"

She laughed before holding up her hand to silence me. "Thank you, Sis. It was a super evening, thanks to you."

I passed a coffee across to her. "So, you've decided things are okay with Jason, then?"

"I reckon so. I just needed time to think, that's all. Things have moved on rather quickly and I'm not good at that. I can't treat relationships as casually as you do."

I peered over the cup that was pressed to my lips. "What are you suggesting?"

"I'm not suggesting anything untoward. I'm simply saying that I've always had a more serious outlook as far as guys are concerned, that's all. I wish I could be different and just enjoy stuff, but I can't."

We chatted in our usual offhand way, flitting from one subject to the next without any obvious connection.

"So, when did Jason contact you?"

I thought. "Monday, I think. He phoned and asked if he could call around and see me – said it was important." I looked Paula in the eye. "He sounded very upset."

"So, what did you tell him?"

"I told him that there was a lot going on and you needed space. Then I suggested the tickets to the show. Sis, he was a lot happier when he left."

"Good. I owe you."

"Don't worry, I have a black book with all the favours you owe me. I might need to get a bigger book the way things are going."

It was good to hear the laugh which had been missing for the last fortnight. "Seriously, he's a proper caring guy that's worth holding on to." Then, fearing the conversation might get too serious, I added, "He's sexy as well."

Paula gave me a satisfied grin. "Are you still seeing Trevor?"

"Who?" I answered.

"Uh, say no more."

"When he came over, Jason asked about me designing some logos for the websites he's working on. I said I'd let him know."

"Really? He never mentioned it to me."

"I suspect after your wonderful evening at the theatre, he had other things on his mind." I laughed. Then turned away as I witnessed the wave of red descend her face. "Come on, Paula, let's go out. I need a change of scenery."

Chapter 30

Matt

Paula and Beverley had appeared at the door for a spontaneous family get-together.

"We were wandering around, so we thought we'd pop in," Paula explained.

"You don't need to give a reason. You know you are more than welcome any time." I reached over and touched her hand.

We were listening to Beverley regaling Emily and me about the foursome night out, when the loud intrusive buzzing of my mobile broke into yet another tale.

I looked at the name: it was Kevin. I took my phone into the kitchen. "Wow, another call from you, and it's not that long since your last one."

"And it's good to speak to you too, Matt." I could picture his grinning face as he spoke.

"I promised I'd phone if I heard any more about the Davieses."

"And you have?" The words were pushed out through clenched teeth as any thought of humour disappeared. "What have you heard?"

"Well, I spoke to an old friend who used to be close to Tracy, many years ago. They used to work together, apparently."

I listened.

"From what I've been told, Tracy had a relationship with some older married man when she was in her early twenties. She became pregnant and the guy she thought was her Heathcliff, her idyllic romantic mate, turned into a violent, vicious bully. One night when he was particularly angry and loud, the neighbours called the police. He did a runner and has never been seen since."

"That's awful. What happened to the baby?"

"Good question. I don't know is the simple answer. But let me finish my story."

"Sorry."

"Apparently, when the police appeared, she was on the floor, blood all over the place, but the baby survived. Tracy was in such a mess mentally, that when the baby was born she was deemed unfit to look after him."

"The baby was a boy?"

"Yes. He was placed into care."

"So, you don't know where he is now?"

"No idea. I don't know if the mother does either. He did go and live with them when he was in his early teens, apparently, but it didn't work out."

Emily appeared at the door and mouthed, "Is everything all right?"

I nodded and she gently pushed the door shut. I was lost in thought as I digested the information.

"Are you still there, Matt?"

"Mm, how old would this baby, boy, man, be now, d'you think?" I asked.

"Let's see. I reckon Tracy was about thirty-five when I met her, at the writing group; so that means she must be around fifty now."

I interjected. "So, her son, whatever he's called, wherever he is, is in his late twenties."

"Okay, you're better at the maths than me."

We concluded the call and I returned to the lounge with scattered thoughts flicking through my brain. I was still in a different world when I felt Emily's eyes fixed on me in concern.

"What's wrong?" asked Paula. "Who was that on the phone?"

I managed to produce a smile. "Just an old friend, nothing to worry about. So, we were talking about your night out?"

Paula turned to Emily. "D'you know what's going on?"

Emily shook her head. "Why don't we all sit down, and relax."

"So, which old friend was it?" she asked gently.

"Kevin."

I watched the colour drain from Paula's face. "There's only one Kevin I've ever heard you mention."

"He's the man that bought Bev an ice cream that day," said Paula quietly. "It is – it's that Kevin, isn't it?" asked Paula, imploring me. "I didn't think you were still in touch, unless it's to do with the Davieses." She paused. "It must be; something's happened, hasn't it?"

I tried hard to appear relaxed and unconcerned as I studied the pensive faces. Three pairs of eyes were fixed on mine as if awaiting a tropical storm.

"Nothing's changed," I said shrugging my shoulders, "but it appears that Tracy has history."

"Go on," said Paula. "That's not enough. What sort of history?"

So, I told them about the violent married man and the baby. Paula gasped and turned to Beverley with a look of horror on her face. "So, this baby – what was it, a boy or girl?"

"It was a boy."

"Then this boy or man as he is now, has connections to the Davieses and might be making some evil plan for us as we speak."

"He could be anyone," said Beverley, her eyes wide in alarm, "or so could the violent father for that matter."

"But…"

Emily interrupted me as she looked across to the girls. "Look, I understand your concern, whenever the Davieses' name

92

is mentioned – I really do. But Kevin was just updating Matt, that's all. Nothing has changed. Everything is the same as last week, last month, last year."

"That's right. He simply promised to phone back if there was any news and that's all he's done." I offered what I hoped was a reassuring smile.

I listened as Paula asked what age the violent womaniser and the son would be, and I told her. "The son would be late twenties and the violent father mid-fifties."

"So, every time we meet men about those ages, we need to be on our guard just in case. That's right, isn't it?" Paula asked, turning towards her sister for confirmation. "We can't trust anyone around those ages."

Emily and I tried desperately hard to get the evening back on an even footing but the damage was done. Even Beverley's laughter and chatter sounded forced.

Chapter 31

Paula

I found myself staring at men over the next few days, causing a few embarrassing moments when the person on the receiving end of my stare wrongly construed my gaze as some sort of physical interest in them. A couple gave me a hopeful smile and approached me. How could I tell them I was interested in their age, and by the way, what was their mother's name?

Eventually the daily ritual of work, plus Jason, listening to Beverley's hectic social life, and get-together's at Uncle Matt's, pushed the Davieses to one side. The work, despite all of my earlier misgivings, I now enjoyed. What I liked most was the feeling of being part of a team, of doing what was best for the company, not just myself. Apart from that, we all seemed to be friends and at the end of the week we got together in the local, for a drink and food.

It was after one of those sojourns that I arrived home happy and relaxed and slumped down on the sofa, ready for a sleepy evening in front of the television.

But those plans were put to one side at the sound of someone hammering on the door. I almost jumped out of my seat. "Who is it?" I asked, making sure the door was still on the latch as I partly opened it.

"Let me in. It's me – I need to talk to you." I found myself staring at the green eyes, ruddy cheeks and lips that I had kissed oh so many times. It was Brendan.

"What the hell are you doing here? You have a nerve."

"Please let me in, it's important." The words were lost on me. It was the closeness of his face and all the memories it conjured up that killed any chance of rational thinking.

"If you don't go away, I'll call the police. NOW – GO!" I shouted as I slammed the door shut.

"*PAULA, PLEASE!*"

"Is that the police?" I shouted. "It is?" I heard an angry bang on the door then the sound of footsteps drifting away into silence. I slumped into a chair and waited a few moments while my loudly beating heart returned to normal. I needed to speak to someone. I searched in my bag for my phone and dialled Jason's number, then cancelled it. What was the point, he didn't know Brendan? I picked up the phone and Beverley answered. "Brendan's been round here," I gasped through the tears that were descending.

"So, what did he want?" asked Beverley when she arrived twenty minutes later.

"I don't know – I frightened him off by pretending to call the police. All I heard was that he had to speak to me about something very important."

"Yeah, yeah. Since he's seen you with Jason, he's realised what a dumbass he's been, screwing around until he lost you. The man's a fool, so don't get taken in by him again. Keep slamming the door in his face, is my suggestion. Either literally or metaphorically, eventually he might get the message." For once the light that usually lit up her face was missing, replaced by a hard glare. "Sis, don't think of the good times you had with him, when you thought he loved you. Remember the heartache and sleepless nights you had at the end when he was cheating on you. That was the real Brendan."

It was some time later when I saw Beverley looking at her watch. "Date, is it?" I inquired innocently.

"Yes, but not in the way that you mean. I have a meeting with your Jason to discuss the work I've done for him and his websites."

"Mm, that explains why he wasn't free this evening. I understand."

"Sis, do you want me to send him round to you after our business has been concluded?"

I laughed, as I usually did with Bev. "No, that's okay. I think we can get by without each other for one evening."

"Then don't start thinking about 'tosser Brendan' for goodness' sake. Think of your loving boyfriend."

Loving Jason came round the following evening for dinner and that was when my world fell apart.

Chapter 32

Jason

"Did you do what you said you were going to do?" asked my friend Steve.

"I did."

The conversation was soon concluded and I went off for my dinner date at Paula's. I tried to appear relaxed, which wasn't easy with my heart hammering. Then her phone buzzed.

"Oh, hi, Bev. Wait, I'll have a look," Paula said.

"What is it?" I asked.

"Bev thinks she may have left her mobile here yesterday."

"You carry on talking, I'll have a look."

I went into the lounge, took her mobile from my pocket, waited thirty seconds, then returned to Paula. "I found it. It was in the back of one of the chairs."

She smiled as I handed it over. "It's here, Bev. Of course, I'll see if you have any urgent messages."

She started to read out a message. "'Yes, it was a wonderful night – one which I will never forget...'" Her voice tailed off as she continued reading.

"*How could you?*" she shrieked at me. "*I thought I meant something to you!*"

"But she encouraged me. It was Beverley who made me. Read her text." I backed away as she read her sister's text to me. I watched the tears begin to flow.

"What's going on?" I heard Beverley shouting out. "What's happening?"

She threw the phone at me. "GET OUT! I NEVER WANT TO SEE YOU AGAIN!"

I watched her on her hands and knees as she picked up the phone and shouted, "WHAT SORT OF SISTER ARE YOU? I NEVER WANT TO SEE YOU EITHER. YOU'RE A SELFISH SLUT! HOW COULD YOU DO THAT TO ME!"

I smiled as I left her house. I knew by heart the text she would have read from Beverley: "Wow – that was special, I will dream about your body until the next time."

The smile soon disappeared and trepidation coursed through me. The next part was going to be oh so difficult to execute. I pressed the doorbell and waited. Matt Bishop came to the door. "Jason, this is a nice surprise. Come on through."

Emily was sitting in the lounge and put her book down and gave me her usual cautious smile. "Would you like a drink?"

I shook my head. "I have something that I had to come and tell you," I hurried out.

"What is it? Is it Paula?" asked Emily, her hand reaching up to her chest.

"It's to do with Paula." I hesitated as they stared at me in alarm. "Well, the truth is I'm leaving the area, and you've made me so welcome that I had to…"

"And what about Paula, is she going, to wherever it is you're going?"

"No, Mrs Bishop, we're not seeing each other any more." My expression was one of abject sorrow as I stared at my feet.

Matt demanded: "What's going on, Jason? We want the truth. You and Paula seemed so happy."

My eyes fixed on Matt's, then looked away. "I'm really sorry that I've been unfaithful."

I heard a gasp from Matt and a knowing nod from Emily. "It wasn't all my fault. I kept saying no but she kept throwing herself at me. Beverley's impossible to resist when she's…"

"BEVERLEY! You were unfaithful with Beverley?" Matt shouted in horror.

"GET OUT!" He moved threateningly towards me.

"Why are you shouting, Dad, and why is Mum crying?" We all turned to the doorway where Harry stood. His pale face was screwed up in uncertainty as he witnessed the rising emotion that filled the room.

Emily moved across to wrap her arms around her son. "We'll talk about it in a minute, love. Jason's in a hurry. He has to be off."

I left, my task complete. I picked up the phone as soon as I arrived at my flat.

"Did it work?" My friend Steve never beat about the bush. He used words sparingly as though he had to pay for them.

"Oh, yes, it worked all right. Tears were flowing in abundance. I'll give you all the gory details tomorrow."

I listened to the chuckling, a sound I rarely heard from him, before disconnecting. The phone rang again immediately. I instinctively went to answer it when my brain kicked in. The only person I would want to speak to was Steve and I had just finished talking to him. I let it ring. 'Buzz, buzz, buzz, buzz.' I tried to ignore it but the sound just filled my head. Eventually the noise stopped and quiet filled the room. I relaxed but not for long as it started again. I looked at the display – it was Beverley. I switched my mobile off and thought about it. She would be coming round here and soon, of that there was no doubt. The only question was, how quickly. I raced to the bedroom and threw clothes into a suitcase. I emptied drawers then hurried into my car. There was only one answer: I would find a hotel to stay at overnight, then go home to Bridgwater.

Chapter 33

Beverley

I was stunned when I heard her launch into Jason, screaming at him to get out. Then she had yelled down the phone at me. *"What sort of sister are you? You're a selfish slut."* From being stunned I spiralled downwards into a state of shock. I tried phoning Jason but there was no answer. I hurried round to Paula's, but as soon as I arrived it was clear that she wasn't there. Her TT was gone and the house was in darkness that echoed the blackness coursing through me. What was going on? I drove on to Uncle Matt and Emily's house where her car had been abandoned across the drive. Now I was going to find out what was going on with my big sister. Had she suffered some sort of mental breakdown? If so, why? I pressed the doorbell and a startled Uncle Matt answered. "Oh, it's you. You'd better come in and explain."

I stepped inside, and the usual feeling of love and affection was missing. Instead I heard sobbing and a mumbled conversation interrupted by wailing. Paula looked up from Emily's comforting hug and gasped. "You – I told you I never wanted to speak or see you again. Get out of the way!"

"Paula," I pleaded. "Stop, we need to talk."

She pushed me to one side, sobbing uncontrollably as she rushed past, before turning and hurling my mobile phone at me. I heard the slamming of the front door as I slumped back against the wall. Tears slid down my face.

"Emily, tell me what's going on. What's wrong with Paula?" I watched Emily struggle to answer, before she looked to Uncle Matt for support.

His tone was unusually harsh. "She said you slept with Jason."

"She said WHAT?! How could she say such a thing?"

Emily blew her nose, "She said she saw texts on your phone that left her in no doubt what was going on."

"THAT'S BULLSHIT! I'd never do such a thing, Uncle Matt, Emily, you cannot believe I'd do such a thing. That's it – I must go and talk to Paula and sort this out." I turned away.

Uncle Matt spoke in a tone that demanded attention. "Beverley, leave it. Paula needs time, she needs space. Leave her be."

"But – it's not true, it's all lies."

I saw Uncle Matt and Emily exchange awkward looks.

"What is it? There's more, isn't there?"

Uncle Matt's eyes hardened. "Jason was round here earlier. He confirmed what Paula said."

My whole body shook in horror.

Emily moved towards me as Uncle Matt continued. "He said that you encouraged him."

Emily drew me into her arms but I felt nothing, only emptiness and bewilderment coursing through me.

I returned home feeling more alone than I had ever felt in my life. I sat down and poured myself a large glass of wine, which I quickly consumed as I tried to understand what had happened. Texts, they said – Jason confirmed it, they said. I jumped out of the chair, grabbed my mobile and scrolled through to messages. I gasped as I read the text from Jason then brought up the text supposedly from me. My shriek shattered the silence before tears started and threatened never to finish. When I eventually staggered down the hallway to my bed, the wine bottle was empty and so was my head. I lay awake, my thoughts focusing on a muddled, drunken plan where I pinned Jason to the ground with a knife at his throat, forcing the truth from him.

Fortunately, that plan was forgotten as I hurried out of bed in the morning with just one idea – to try once more to see Jason. My stomach would only cope with black coffee, which I gulped down and then started the car. I arrived at his flat and pressed the doorbell, again and again. No answer. I tried his phone: no answer.

Chapter 34

Jason

As I drove along the motorway towards home, the vision of anger and tears as I left the Bishop household kept launching itself in front of me. A picture of Matt's contorted face as he shouted, "Get out" loomed as I drove too close to the lorry dawdling in front of me. My foot hit the brake. I HAD SUCEEDED! I HAD INFLICTED PAIN!

When I first set off on my mission many months ago, I had severe doubts about my ability to achieve what I'd been asked to do, but to my amazement I'd done everything and more. I had shattered the loving family life, placed a large boulder between Paula and Beverley, and now tears were the norm rather than laughter. BRILLIANT!

I looked forward to seeing the smile crease the face of my friend Steve when I recounted yesterday's events. But there was also the loving couple I felt were almost like parents to me, and that's when my euphoria drained away.

I had arrived home, emptied my cases and collapsed onto the sofa. That's when there was a knock on the door.

"Well done!" said Steve as he gave me a hug. "I thought we should celebrate, so I brought this." He produced a bottle of whisky. "Tell me all." So, I did.

"You did well, really well. I'm proud of you."

"Thanks, but they'll get over it. It might take a while, but they're a close family, and they'll find a way."

"I know, I know. I'm thinking of the next stage now. I need to find a way of ruining Matt Bishop's reputation in the business sector. I haven't thought it through yet, but I will."

"How's Gordon?" I inquired. That's when the smile disappeared.

"Not good. He doesn't have much longer, but the terrible thing is, he doesn't seem to care. He smiles and laughs as though he hasn't a care in the world, and Liz is the same. They both go on about it being God's will, I ask you."

I took a swig of whisky. "I keep thinking back to when I first moved here, how they made me feel so welcome, so at home. Rather different to what I'd been used to, that's for sure. He transformed my life."

"Jason, don't. We've been through all of that, and what he did for me. There's nothing to be gained by going over it again and again. That's why you went to Malvern to cause havoc and it worked. But it's only the start."

Lying in bed after Steve had left, my thoughts began to wander. The story I'd told Paula of my early years was true. They were difficult, to say the least. If I hadn't had help when I came to Bridgwater, it could so easily have ended in disaster. But it was utopia compared to the awful life that Steve had to live when growing up. He'd shared his desperate tale with me one evening when I was complaining about my lot, and at the end I'd felt humbled and embarrassed.

He had been passed around foster parents for many years before his real parents took him in. As he grew older, he increasingly found living with Dan and Tracy strange and empty. The house felt devoid of any love or affection. At just eighteen Steve had left and gone to live near Dan's brother Gordon, who had just been released from prison. There, for the first time, he found adults he could trust and rely on. I remembered the tale Steve had told me about Gordon finding out about his shoplifting habit. He'd been taken back to the shop and made to apologise for accidentally leaving the premises without paying. "He asked me to promise that I would never shoplift again, and I didn't. I couldn't," he told me. "He trusted me and I couldn't let him down." He also told me about the first time he met Gordon and stole money from his wallet. The next day Gordon appeared and asked if he needed any more money for his drug habit. He never stole or did drugs again.

But early on, I couldn't stop myself from asking Gordon about prison. What was it like? Why was he there? He explained with absolute sadness that he deserved to be locked up, and changed the subject. Of course, I couldn't leave it alone. "But what did you do?" I persisted. Reluctantly he told me about his fiancée at that time and how Emily had given him her engagement ring back and they had split. What happened with Matt Bishop he glossed over but took full responsibility for it and his incarceration.

We became closer to Gordon through the local football team, the choir and anything to do with the community. It seemed inconceivable that such a Christian man should have been denied so many years of proper life, stuck behind bars. Then as the early signs of his illness took hold, our hatred for the people responsible for destroying his life grew.

I struggled to sleep that night and woke feeling tired and ill at ease as I met up with Steve to visit Liz and Gordon. Whilst I had been away, Steve had intentionally kept a distance from them as he feared questions about what I was up to in Malvern. He had long ago learnt that Gordon had an instinctive way of sensing any kind of wrongdoing. We knocked on the door and I had a curious foreboding about what was to come as I saw the uncertainty on Liz's usually contented face.

"I'll just check that he's okay to see you."

Steve and I exchanged worried looks while we waited.

Liz came back. "He's fine. You can go in, but it's best if you don't stay too long. I should warn you, his speech isn't brilliant at the moment, so be aware of that. Follow me. His bedroom has been moved into the living room. Don't stay too long," she repeated.

We entered his new bedroom. Gordon sat up and greeted us with a smile and a garbled, "Mon nin, ate to see uw."

Steve answered, "You too."

I couldn't speak as I stared at the face in front of me. The hair was white, the expression lost. I turned away and focused on the table pushed into the corner. We had spent many happy hours playing all sorts of silly card games on that table.

Steve said sharply, "Don't you agree, Jason?" I turned back, but Gordon's eyes were lost, gazing off into the distance as if in a trance. It wasn't too long before we said goodbye, saying we would visit him again soon.

It was a quiet journey home, both of us lost in our own private thoughts. As I got out of the car, Steve said, "It's all down to that Matt Bishop and that tart Emily. They will suffer, oh how they'll suffer. What you did was only the start."

I didn't answer. There was nothing more to be said.

Chapter 35

Beverley

It was all lies! Lies! But that didn't matter. The truth was, it had destroyed our family. Whenever I tried to phone Paula, it would just ring and ring, or the message on her answerphone would play. When I went round to her house the door was always locked. What was going on? Why had Jason told Uncle Matt and Emily that I'd slept with him? What was the purpose behind that evil, despicable confabulation? Whenever I tried to talk to Uncle Matt or Emily the subject was closed. They'd promised Paula they wouldn't discuss it with me.

My mind was in turmoil. I threw myself into different work projects, with men and dates most definitely off the menu for the foreseeable future. I phoned home, but I rarely visited. I couldn't face the looks from Uncle Matt and Emily, the disapproval and awkwardness instead of the love that I had taken for granted.

I kept thinking about the texts and in particular the one that I had supposedly sent to Jason. My phone had gone missing and it had been found at Paula's, so logically the text had to have been forged by either Paula or Jason.

Could it have been Paula – NO WAY! That meant it had to be Jason, but why? If he wanted to split from Paula, there were easier ways, that's for sure. Then he disappeared and his mobile kept churning out that infuriating message: "number not recognised". But why on earth would he make up such evil lies? What could he possibly have achieved by that?

I sat staring at the coffee as I stirred the creamy antiseptic, oblivious to the noise going on around me.

"It's Paula's sister, isn't it? I'm sorry, I don't remember your name."

I looked up to see an intelligent face with piercing eyes I recognised but couldn't put a name to. "Oh, hi," I mumbled.

He held out his hand. "It's Simon, Simon Roach – Paula's old boss. We met at last year's Christmas party."

"Of course! It's Beverley." There was an awkward silence before he spoke again.

"It's timely that I bumped into you. D'you mind?" He indicated the seat opposite me.

"Please."

"I had a visit last night at work, just as I was about to leave. Someone called Brendan? He was looking for Paula."

My shoulders slumped. That's all we needed.

"I simply told him that she wasn't there and that I was about to lock up." I noticed that though the gentle smile stayed in place, those penetrating eyes were fixed on mine as he continued. "The young man looked most distraught and said that it was of the utmost importance that he talk to her."

I watched Roach stand up. "If you think it's important, perhaps you could pass it on to Paula. Give her my regards."

I watched him walk away. Pass the message on to Paula, he'd said. If only. How could I when she wouldn't speak to me? Besides, how important could it be when it was that louse Brendan wanting to get back together with Paula? What had she done to deserve such lousy, despicable men?

I made up my mind and went round to see Uncle Matt and Emily.

"Oh, hi. Come on in." For the first time I noticed the lines around Uncle Matt's eyes. I'd always seen him as kind, gentle and ageless. Everything was changing. When Emily appeared with her usual bright smile and warm hug, her paleness hit me.

"I bumped into Paula's old boss, Simon Roach earlier." I told them what Roach had said. "So, if you pass it on to Paula when you see her next, and she can decide whether she wants to see Brendan or not. It's up to her."

I watched them nod and felt lost and alone. "I KEEP TELLING YOU I DID NOTHING!" I yelled. "WHY DOES NO ONE BELIEVE ME?" The tears began to fall again and I hurried towards the door.

"Darling, please, don't go – we need to talk." Emily put her arm around me and pulled me gently back.

"Bev, we do believe you," said Uncle Matt, "but we're lost. We don't understand any of this. What did Jason gain by these lies?"

"He's made us all unhappy," I sniffed. "That's what."

Chapter 36

Paula

Did I really believe that my sister had slept with Jason? There was no doubting it from the texts I'd read, and furthermore, Jason categorically said he had. But after the initial shock had waned, I wasn't so sure. I'd seen the wonder in his eyes when he'd set eyes on her for the first time. I wasn't offended or surprised; I'd seen that look many times before. But even if he hadn't slept with her, he'd wanted to. He wanted her more than me, and that's what really hurt. All those soft, murmured words about me being the only girl for him, and the many times we lay cuddled up together, when he told me he loved me. They were just words, meaningless words, no connection with reality.

Fortunately, I had work and I threw myself hard enough into it that I could forget my love life, or lack of it, for a few hours a day. Brian James called me into his office one morning. "Paula, are you free Thursday evening?"

I forced a smile. "That depends?"

"Have a read."

It was an email from Simon Roach.

> Margaret Schultz is leaving at the end of this week and we are having a bit of a send-off in The Red Lion after work on Thursday. If any of your staff would like to come along, they will be most welcome.

I looked at Brian. "Sorry, I'm busy – can't make it."

His head tilted to one side as he looked questioningly at me.

I sighed. "All right, that isn't totally true. The fact is, Margaret Schultz never liked me and did her best to turn the others against me, so why would I want to give her a happy send-off?"

"Mm, I see. Well, if you change your mind, just turn up. I know Simon Roach will be there and I know he wanted a quiet word, preferably in person."

"That settles it. I definitely won't be there." I stood up.

"Paula, you're wrong about Simon. He believes in you and has your best interests at heart."

I mumbled something and left his office. I tried not to give it any more thought – why would I? My unhappy time at Walker Investments while Simon Roach was in charge was a thing of the past, and as for Schultz, why would I want to see her again, let alone party with her?

Driving back from Bromsgrove on Thursday though, I started to have doubts. I couldn't help wondering how Deborah and some of the other girls were doing, and both Colin and Brian seemed to think that Simon Roach was someone to be trusted. So, should I find out what he wanted to see me about?

I parked the car, entered The Red Lion and stood just inside the door, surveying the scene. Margaret's voice dominated the room. "Of course, things were better after Paula Carter left. It was no longer all about her and how brilliant she was. Selfish bitch, everyone was secondary to her."

A male voice broke into her rant. "You don't know what you're talking about. Paula's not like that at all – she is the most thoughtful and caring person you can imagine."

I recognised the impassioned voice immediately and looked across to see the angry face of Brendan.

"I thought I recognised you. You're her ex, aren't you? Is that

111

why you dumped her for someone else, because she's so thoughtful?"

Angela reached over and put her hand on his arm. "We should go, Brendan – this is a private party. We'll go somewhere else."

He hesitated. I saw him open his mouth to say something, change his mind then stand up and look towards the door where I was standing.

I turned to leave. "Paula!" he shouted. "I need to speak to you."

I didn't look back as I hurried away. What a mistake I'd made coming here.

Brendan appeared at my side. "Paula, it's about Jason. Please?"

The tears began to flow. "I can't, I can't talk." I opened my car door.

"Oh, Paula, we really need to talk. He's not who you thought he was. Can I come round tomorrow?

The gentle tones were too much. I nodded and drove off.

I'd forgotten just how nasty Margaret Schultz was. If anything, the bitter way she had described me was a more accurate portrayal of herself. But what she was good at was manipulating people, and no doubt all the other staff felt the same about me. The following morning Brian James appeared at my desk.

"I've just got a couple of coffees. D'you want to join me? So," – he leaned back in his chair – "Simon told me about last night and Schultz's vitriolic outburst."

I looked away. It was pointless to say anything.

"Oh, don't worry, I know the score. Between you and me, Simon is pleased that she's leaving. It makes life easier, and don't repeat that."

"I didn't get the chance to speak to Roach."

"I know, that's why he wanted me to talk to you and put you in the picture."

I swallowed hard. "What about?"

"He wants you to return to his Birmingham branch now that Schultz has left."

Chapter 37

Paula

I opened the door to stare into a face I knew so well. Even the lines across his forehead and the uncertainty in his eyes didn't undermine just how handsome he was. I ushered him in, and he sat at the kitchen table as I poured a cup of coffee and placed it in front of him. A smidgeon of milk and one sugar.

"Thank you for sticking up for me with that bitch Schultz," I started.

"Paula, I need to tell you about Angela…"

I held up my hand. "Stop – now. You're here to tell me about Jason. You said it was important."

"But…"

The dam burst as I stood up. "YOU CAN LEAVE NOW IF YOU'RE NOT GOING TO LISTEN TO ME!"

"All right, it is important," he sighed. "I was in The Red Lion about a month ago. In fact, I was outside when I saw Jason walk in, with this rather hideous smirk on his face. A few minutes later I heard him on his phone. He couldn't see me," he explained, "'cause my chair was round to the side.

"'Steve,' I heard him say, 'I've come up with the plan to destroy the closeness of the family and leave them loathing one another.' It went quiet for a while, then he said, 'I just need to get hold of her mobile.' He wandered away, laughing, out of earshot, but it sounded very sinister. I've been trying to tell you this for ages."

I slumped back in my chair, feeling lost and afraid.

"Are you all right, Paula? You look pale." He reached across to take my hand, but instinctively I moved away.

"Thanks, Brendan – it's very good of you to let me know. I should have listened to you before. I'm sorry I didn't – it would have saved a lot of heartache." I pushed my chair away. "I have to go."

"Paula, what's going on? I want to help?"

"No, Brendan. You've been very helpful already. I must go and see Beverley straight away." I finally gazed into those green eyes. "I wish you and Angela all the best."

I knocked on Beverley's door and waited. The curtains were pulled back as Beverley's inquisitive face peered out. Moments passed then the door opened.

"Hi," she said guardedly.

What could I expect? A month had drifted by since we had last talked, if shouting could be termed talking. "I've come to apologise – I got everything wrong."

She still looked unsure as she stepped aside and let me in.

"So, you believe me now? Really, the sister who has always had your best interests at heart, who has always looked out for you – who you didn't trust or believe? Instead you believed a lying asshole?"

I nodded, too embarrassed to speak.

My sister's lively, energetic face was still missing. "Tell me – why the change? What's happened?"

So, I told her what Brendan had said.

"So, we were set up and Jason was nothing but a lying toe rag." She moved towards me and hugged me. "You must feel awful, the bastard. How can anyone be so evil? Why?"

"Bev, I feel like shit for the way I treated you. I'll never forgive myself."

"Paula, it's…"

"Wait! It's not that I didn't believe you when you said you hadn't slept with him, but I'm sure he wanted you more than he wanted me. That's what I couldn't cope with. I thought I had finally found someone I could trust after Brendan, but how wrong could I be? All I found was that when it comes to men I haven't a clue. They're all cheating, lying, untrustworthy bastards."

"Sis, there's a wonderful guy out there waiting to meet you," she said earnestly.

I shrugged.

"But don't you think it's ironic that it was Brendan who found out what was going on?"

I conjured up a superficial smile. "But why, Bev? Why this devious, underhanded, dastardly plot?"

My sister answered without thinking. "To bring unhappiness into our family, it seems, and they achieved it."

While I was still with Beverley, I phoned home. "Can Beverley and I come over tomorrow evening for a chat if you and Uncle Matt are around?"

There was a pause, then a cautious, "Is everything all right?"

"Yes, everything is fine between us. I was such a fool, but we need to talk to you about what went on."

"Oh, thank goodness for that – at long last. Yes, of course you can."

We chatted some more, before hanging up.

Chapter 38

Paula

Uncle Matt poured some wine and we sloped off to the lounge. "Harry's upstairs doing homework, so leave him be for the moment. Tell Emily and me what's been going on."

I looked at Beverley. "Firstly, I have been such a fool and I can't tell you how awful I feel about the way I've behaved."

"Sis, that's not important any more. Tell them what Brendan told you."

"Brendan? You did say Brendan, didn't you? Where does he fit into this?" A puzzled expression crossed Emily's face.

"Yes, Brendan. He came round and told me what he overheard Jason telling someone."

"What? What did he hear?" asked Uncle Matt.

After I had told them, I watched their faces cloud over as they slumped back in their chairs, trying to take in what I had said.

"We were set up," explained Beverley. "Someone wanted to hurt us big time."

"Why would anyone do such a despicable thing?" asked Emily.

"The question is," interrupted Uncle Matt, "who was Jason...or whoever he really is, who was he was talking to? Has he mentioned any friends, from wherever it is he came from?"

"That's a point," said Emily. "Where did he come from?"

I tried to get my battered brain into gear. "I know he originated from Bromsgrove – I'm sure that's what he told me. Then he moved down south, but where to I've no idea."

"Think," encouraged Matt.

"I don't think he said." With all eyes on me I felt as though I had failed. "I'm sure he never said."

Uncle Matt stood up and began pacing the room. "There's only one family evil enough to orchestrate what happened, and that's the Davieses. There's no alternative."

"But why? Why now? It can't be Gordon Davies – Liz said he had Parkinson's. Besides, according to her he's a changed man – he's found God. Anyway, where does Jason fit into all of this? What's the link?" Emily picked up the bottle of wine and began topping up.

Beverley looked questioningly at me.

"There's no point asking me – I don't know him. I never knew him – that much is clear."

It went quiet as we mulled over the possibilities.

"How about," began Matt as he put his hand on Emily's, "you give Liz Potter a ring and find out if she knows anything about Jason?"

My heart began to pound as a thought burst into my head, shattering any semblance of calm. "Jason is twenty-five," I blurted out.

It went quiet, as they took this in. "D'you think…?" asked Beverley breathlessly.

"He could be Tracy's son that Kevin told me about?" Uncle Matt uttered the words that were in our heads but we refused to let free.

Emily added in a measured tone, "I'll phone Liz tomorrow and see if she knows anything about Jason."

A gentle voice interrupted our thoughts: "I've finished my homework."

We looked towards the doorway to see the fresh, innocent face of Harry.

"Hi, Harry," I said, reaching over to give him a hug.

"What are you talking about? You all looked very serious."

"Oh, nothing important," said Emily. "We've finished now."

Chapter 39

Paula

"Damn, who is that now?" That was the last thing I needed. I ignored it and carried on reading, but the knocking continued. I put my book down, though in truth I had absorbed nothing of what I had read, and strode to the door. I opened it and took a step back in surprise. It was Angela Moore.

"I hope you don't mind, but I need to speak to you." Although I had heard her speak before, her voice had never been directed at me. In fact, the only contact had been me glaring at her accusingly, if that could be termed communication.

"May I?" She pushed past me and walked through to the kitchen and sat down.

"Why are you here? What d'you want?" It was the first time I had been up close to her. Usually my glare was from a distance. Now up close, to my annoyance, I could see she had a gentle, friendly face.

I could see her thinking. "I said…" I continued angrily.

"It's about Brendan."

Of course it was about Brendan. What else could it be about? "He…"

My hand flew to my mouth in horror. "Nothing's happened to him, has it?"

She smiled. "He's fine. It's just that he told me that he's tried to talk to you – I mean about me and him but you won't listen."

"Spare me." I stood up and retrieved my coffee.

"It's not what you think. We are not a couple," she rushed out as she stared at me, but I just gave her a wry, disbelievingly stare back. "Please, this is important."

I sat back down and studied my watch. "Right, you have five minutes then I want your backside out of here."

"Could I have a drink of water?"

"Help yourself."

She sat back down and started. "Brendan is my half-brother, which means we haven't, wouldn't, you know…"

My lips puckered in disgust. "Wow, as lies go that's not a bad one."

Angela shot me an unnerving glare. "Believe me, it's the truth and it's not a nice story. Listen, Brendan's father left him and his wife, and formed a relationship with my mother and I was the result. Before he knew about me he returned to his proper family. He died a few years later without knowing of my existence. In fact, I never knew I had a half-brother until about eighteen months ago, when my mother decided to tell me the true story, rather than the one she had fabricated. That was a special gift for my coming-of-age birthday. What d'you think of that, eh? Not many people get a gift like that for their twenty-first."

I leaned forward, my interest piqued. "Go on, what happened next?"

"I found Brendan's location online easily enough, then I spent days, and nights," she grimaced, "working out how to arrange a meet-up. I just couldn't bring myself to write to him and say, 'I'm your sister and would like to get together and chat?' I just couldn't."

"So, what did you do?"

She lifted her glass. "Have you anything stronger?"

I found a bottle of wine and poured two glasses and as I handed one to her I found myself studying her. Were there any similarities between her and Brendan? I knew his face so well. After all, I had lain beside him many times, gazing lovingly at him. Angela's ears were slightly large, as were Brendan's. Did that mean anything?

Angela saw what I was doing and smiled. "D'you see any likeness?"

I ignored her. "So, what did you do?"

"I couldn't think of any intelligent ideas, so I tried plan B."

"Go on, I'm listening. What was plan B?"

Angela's eyes lit up. "I just turned up on his doorstep."

"No! What did he say?" I watched as the gentle smile lit up her face. Perhaps she wasn't the evil person Beverley and I had talked about in disparaging 'whore' terms.

"I asked if he could spare ten minutes as there was something really important I had to see him about. Once inside I showed him a photo that I'd got from my mother. Brendan looked very confused and asked who it was. He disappeared upstairs and came back with an album which he flicked through. There were a number of photos of his father. He went very quiet for what seemed like ages, then he blurted out, 'Why have you got a photo of my father?'"

"Because he's my father as well," I told him.

"Poor Brendan, how did he take it? Did he believe it?"

"He believed it. He just stared at the photo, then asked me to leave some contact details. He needed time to get his head round it, he said.

"Paula, I really wanted to give him a big hug. He looked shell-shocked, but I was afraid it might tip him over the edge."

"So, what happened next?"

"Well, a few days later he contacted me and we met up. He'd confronted his mother and she had admitted that Brendan's dad had left her and formed a relationship with some floozy at some point, and…" She paused and emptied her glass. "Before my mum told me about my half-brother and the truth about my father, she wrote to Brendan's mother and told her about me."

"Wow, what a nightmare."

"Not the best. Brendan told me that his mother was insistent that our – how shall I put it – 'family connection' should remain private."

I couldn't help it – I took Angela's hand in mine. "I feel for you."

Chapter 40

Matt

Emily and I talked into the early hours, then we both tossed and turned.

"How can I ring Liz Potter and casually drop Jason into the conversation?" Emily asked. "Oh by the way, do you know a Jason Brown? He's been driving a wedge in our family with his lies and deceit, and the only person capable of doing that is someone with links to the Davieses. And yes, Liz, I know you're married to Gordon Davies, but I always think of you as Liz Potter."

I could see Emily was tired and morose when I woke up later that morning and slowly drank my coffee.

"Are you going to do it?" I asked.

She nodded. "In a minute."

I watched as she finished her breakfast and hesitantly picked up the phone. 'Ring, ring, ring, ring.' No answer. She tried five times that day, but no answer. The following morning she was about to try again, when the postman pushed a letter through the door. It was addressed to Emily. Her forehead creased in thought as she stared at the vaguely familiar-looking writing. She tore the envelope open and read, open-mouthed.

"What is it?" I asked, seeing her shocked expression.

"It's Liz, Liz Potter. She says Gordon has gone – he's died." Emily passed me the letter. "After her last email it's probably a relief to them both, if you see what I mean."

I nodded, and read. "So, she's gone over to Cyprus to stay

123

with Dan and Tracy. I suppose they are her brother- and sister-in-law, after all."

"Ye-es, but I'm not sure what sort of influence they'll have on her. But it does mean I can't talk to her about Jason until she gets back."

"I know. Nothing is ever simple with that lot, that's for sure."

Over the next few days, while the bright yellow sun stared down from above there was always the feeling of dark clouds gathering, ready to unleash themselves on us. I felt we were in a state of limbo. Then the phone rang.

"It's Peter Ryder, for you, Matt, and he sounds most agitated," Emily whispered. Peter was an ex-work colleague of mine from when I was working at Edwards Little & Co. a few years ago. We still kept in touch.

"Have you seen tonight's *Gazette*?" he shouted angrily before I could speak.

"No, we don't get the local paper," I explained.

"I suggest you look online straight away. Ring me back when you do," he demanded, leaving me staring at the phone in disbelief as the line went dead. Peter was a quiet, unaggressive friend who rarely displayed any kind of annoyance. I quickly fired up my laptop brought up the *Gazette* website and read.

I couldn't believe it! Why on earth…? I was in a different world, staring up at the ceiling, when Emily placed a cup of coffee in front of me.

"What's wrong?" Emily immediately noted the despair and confusion.

I thrust the laptop and the vicious, lying, evil review in front of her. There was a photo of David Newman by the header.

"Wasn't he one of your clients?" Emily inquired.

"Unfortunately, yes," I snarled. "Read it."

"*Don't make the same mistake as me,*" it started. "*I made a nearly catastrophic error when I sought financial guidance and used an accountancy company that was not up to the standard I required. To compound it, when a certain individual left I continued to use him, because I was too loyal. It took three whole years to recover from those mistakes."*

"Matt?"

"It's all lies. A certain individual! It's obvious to everyone he means me! The only reason he struggled was because: one, he didn't put the time into Newman Motors, and two, he took out more money than the company could afford. I kept telling him that."

Emily's hand reached out for mine. "He doesn't mention your name or Edwards Little & Co."

"I know love, but everybody in the business community knows which accountancy company he used and who he's referring to." I gazed into the distance, seeking inspiration. "I'd better ring Peter Ryder."

"Matt, sit down." She placed a cup of coffee in front of me. "You're too wound up. You need to calm down and think straight before you speak to Ryder."

"But why has he come out with something so outrageous after all this time? It doesn't make sense."

It was some minutes later when I phoned my ex-work colleague. "Well, what d'you think?" His voice was only marginally less loud and venomous.

I replied, "It's really weird. Okay, it's a pack of lies, but why now? What's the point?"

"I'm not interested in why, I just know it's scandalous and we should sue the ass off him."

"How can we, he doesn't mention any names? In fact, it's very cleverly done, which sounds beyond David Newman. He's too thick to think up anything clever."

"Huh, we can't just sit back and accept it. Whatever the

reason, it's caused no end of damage to my reputation and yours. I've already had former clients ringing me and I've had to laugh it off and pretend it's of no concern."

"Peter, I'm just as angry, confused and outraged as you, but, perhaps it's best if we think about it. How about we give it a couple of days then get together. What d'you reckon?"

I almost pictured his shoulders slump. "That's probably a good idea. We need to find a way of getting a retraction from him."

Chapter 41

Paula

"How's things, Bev? Work good, boyfriends in abundance as usual?" I'd met up with Beverley in The Fox and was determined to focus on what was happening in her life rather than the helter-skelter affair that was mine.

"Yeah, everything's good with me. What about you?"

"Oh, so-so. Have you spoken to Uncle Matt or Emily in the last couple of days?" I asked as we sat down.

"No, I've had too much on. Why? Any news on the dastardly Davieses?"

"No, it's nothing to do with that lot. Emily said that Uncle Matt has been absolutely furious with some guy who wrote a review in the *Gazette* which undermined him and the company he used to work for. And, to make it worse, someone wrote another review backing it up."

"No, you're kidding me? No wonder he's furious. Why would anyone do that?"

"I don't know and neither does he, but he's determined to get to the bottom of it."

Beverley leaned forward. "Apart from Uncle Matt, what's bothering you?"

"Everything's fine, I told you."

"Yes, and I'm a multimillionaire brain surgeon."

"Uh?"

"You're telling porkies." She flicked hair out of her eyes

and stared at me.

"Oh, all right. So much for a nice quiet evening out with no aggro. Finish your drink – I'll get another."

Beverley smiled. "I see. It's as bad as that, is it?"

I went to the bar and looked around. It was quiet, which was perfect, as I didn't think I could cope with noise or bustle. My brain needed downtime, or perhaps it needed my sister.

I placed the glass in front of her and she sat upright. "Tell me?"

"There's nothing life-threatening. It's just that I've been asked to go back to Birmingham, working for Simon Roach, and I don't know what to do."

"I thought you were happy in Bromsgrove working with what's-his-name, Brian James."

I watched as two teenagers cast their heads sideways to stare at Beverley before moving to the bar.

"I am happy at Bromsgrove. They're a lovely crowd to work with, but at Colin's place, I mean Simon Roach's – slip of the tongue, that – the work was more demanding, more rewarding, and I don't mean financially."

"I think you've made your mind up, Paula."

I pondered. "I think perhaps you're right."

"What else is going on with you?"

"Well…"

"Uh, uh, when you start with a 'well' I know it's serious."

I couldn't help but laugh. "When did you become so perceptive? For years I looked out for you. Now, much to my chagrin, it's the other way around. It will change again, you mark my words."

"Yeah, yeah, but back to now. You started with a 'well'."

"Okay, well, the other evening, you'll never guess who came to see me."

Beverley gazed up at the ceiling then shook her head. "Tell me."

128

"Angela Moore." I watched the sharp intake of breath.

"Never – what did that whore want, contraceptive pills?"

"Beverley, behave yourself – she's all right. We misjudged her."

"Really?" she asked with a wry, disbelieving curl of her lips.

"Really. They're not a couple. They're not sleeping together." I gave my best open and frank expression.

"They're just friends then, are they? That's such bullshit – what planet are you on? Brendan and Angela Whore not shagging?" Come on, Paula, get real."

"Trust me, it's true."

"Paula, you are so gullible."

The word gullible hit me as I thought of Jason. "I know I am," I said dejectedly, "but this time know that I'm right. I can't tell you how I know, but I am."

Beverley sighed. "Okay, I won't pry. But is that why she came to see you, to tell you that she and Brendan were just friends?"

"Partly. She also told me that Brendan had gone to her for support, ages ago, because his girlfriend" – I pointed a finger at my chest – "had problems and wasn't able to commit."

Angela had explained in a gentle, caring voice. "He told me that he loved you, but something stopped you from giving yourself emotionally. He said that you were always holding back, that you were afraid."

Those words had never been far from my mind since they were gently lobbed at me, and as I repeated them to Beverley, the impact hit me once more, and I felt an icy coldness descend.

Beverley paused before asking, "Are you going to get back together with Brendan?"

The question seemed to appear from a distance. "Are you all right, Sis?" She looked at me in concern.

"Can we change the subject, please? Can we talk about anything other than me?"

Chapter 42

Paula

"It sounds like Uncle Matt is in a bad place at the moment. I think you should go and see him – you're so good at giving support," Beverley had said. I knew my sister was trying to distract me, but as I entered the house and saw Emily, my own problems went into temporary hiding. "Have I caught you at a bad time?"

"I was just leaving. I'm meeting up with Uncle Matt for lunch. Have you eaten?"

"Not yet, no."

"Perfect, you can join us." She smiled, but the lines on her forehead still dominated.

We entered the café and found a seat. "How is Uncle Matt doing? Has he sorted out the issue with his old client?"

"He went off to see Peter Ryder this morning. He was an old work colleague at Edwards Little & Co.," she explained, "and he's beside himself."

"Who's beside themselves, Uncle Matt or this Ryder fellow?"

Emily gave a wry grin. "Sorry, I think both."

I looked up to see a man abstractedly pushing open the door and almost knocking over an old lady, who was leaving. Uncle Matt humbly offered his apologies as she glared at him before exiting.

"I didn't see her." His eyes were wide and troubled. "Oh, hi Paula, good to see you.

"Did you see?" he continued.

"Matt, it was an accident and nobody was hurt. Forget it. Now, how did your meeting go?" asked Emily.

He turned towards me. "Have you heard about the newspaper article and letter?" His eyes had this haunted look.

"Yeah, Bev told me about it. It's awful – I can't understand why anyone would want to do that."

He picked up the coffee that was in front of him. "That's what Ryder keeps saying: 'Why would Newman write such a pack of lies?'"

"Have you come up with any possible reasons?" I asked.

"None whatsoever. All I know is that when I go to the tennis club my so-called friends feel awkward around me. I feel a bit like a pariah, and Peter said he's stopped going to his golf club, because he doesn't feel comfortable any more. I know it sounds daft, but he'd been a member for twenty-odd years and now he feels embarrassed."

"D'you think that was the intention?"

I sensed two pairs of eyes staring at me and felt strangely self-conscious.

"I mean, this toe rag who wrote the newspaper review has caused grief and heartache and he must have known that would be the outcome." I stopped and thought. "Which means that for whatever reason, perhaps that was the intention."

It went quiet, then Uncle Matt's eyes lit up as he looked towards the counter and latched onto a portly man.

"Matt!" Emily shouted as he leapt from his seat and rushed towards the man, tapping him excitedly on the shoulder.

"David, how good to bump into you."

"What the…?" The blood drained from the man's face. "Matt Bishop, what are you doing here?" His eyes furtively looked towards the door.

Matt ignored the question. "I've been trying to get hold of you for days, but you're always busy apparently. Why did you

131

write that review? I need some answers." I watched him move behind Newman and block the exit.

"Sir, I'm afraid you're disturbing the other customers." Matt saw the worried expression from the uniformed man behind the counter.

"Why?" persisted Matt.

"I was told to. I had no choice." He shook his arm free and pushed past Matt and out through the exit.

Uncle Matt returned to his seat impervious to the stares and whispers of the other customers. "Did you hear him? Did you hear what he said? He had no choice. He was told to? I'm at a total loss to know what's going on."

Chapter 43

Paula

It had been a stressful lunch, afternoon and evening as the 'I was told to' was analysed, dissected then reanalysed, until we were all too tired to think any more. But all of that was pushed aside as I focused on my return to the Birmingham branch of Walkers.

Simon Roach called me into his office immediately I arrived. I walked past all the other girls, who had their heads down, concentrating hard as I walked towards his office. I sat in the offered seat, my head full of the last two less-than-joyful meetings in this intimidating office.

"Delighted you're back with us," said Roach, breaking into my reverie. "Brian James told me what an excellent job you'd done in Bromsgrove and that he was sorry to see you go."

I forced a smile, suspicious of this new friendly Roach as he talked non-stop for the next half an hour. Even his eyes betrayed an unlikely degree of warmth.

"Business has been good but that's due in the main to an upturn in the economy. Now the experts are predicting a downturn and we need everyone to pull together."

"Pull together, pull together," the words buzzed around my head as I returned to my desk.

Throughout the week I made a point of smiling and being friendly. On Friday I had lunch with Deborah at a nearby café, as I was keen to get her onside to encourage the others to be positive. As we waited for our food, I was aware that she was slightly on edge.

I tried to put her at ease. "Uncle Matt told me many moons ago how he first met my mum – my birth mum, that is."

Deborah peered across at me.

"Apparently my mum was in charge of a few of the staff in the kindergarten where she worked. They used to all go to a local pub at the end of the working week for a sort of informal review of the week – an excuse to have a drink, I suspect. That's where Uncle Matt met her for the first time, and then he turned up every Friday until they got together. My mum had to ask him out as he was too frightened to, apparently."

Deborah laughed. "What a soppy story, but not a happy ending?"

I smiled. "It was, but not together. But I think we should do the same."

"You think some guy will ask us out?" Deborah laughed once more.

"No, I mean, we should all wander down to The Lamb and Flag after work on a Friday and have a no-holds-barred chat about the week. Just an amiable get-together, good for team building. What d'you think?"

Deborah's lips creased into a straight line and she averted her eyes.

"Deb, please, try and convince the others. I really want us to pull together and work as a team. Are you with me?"

She stared cautiously at me. "I'm with you but the others feel awkward because they treated you so badly when you were here before, you know, what with Margaret Schultz pulling all the strings."

"Oh her – say no more. Ah, here's the food." I looked her in the eye. "Tell the others not to worry about the past. We need to move on. Besides, I deserved a lot of the criticism then, but I've changed for the better."

She didn't answer but the following Friday as soon as work

finished, we trundled down to The Lamb and Flag and discussed the good, the bad and the ugly of the working week. Apart from the interaction, they enjoyed the free drink that I donated to encourage the success of the evening.

Inevitably, the name Margaret Schultz cropped up. "So, where is she working now?" I inquired in an attempt to show a degree of interest I didn't feel.

"She's working at her uncle's corner shop," someone replied.

"Wow, that's a bit of a comedown," I commented.

"But it's only temporary until the baby arrives," came another voice.

"Huh, so she's pregnant, is she? Well, there's a surprise. Does anyone, including her, know who the father is?" I laughed.

"Yes, it's Jason – Jason Brown," answered Molly.

The glass of wine slipped from my fingers and smashed to the floor.

"Is that a definite?" I asked, the words just audible through barely functioning lips.

"Yes, she's sure. That's right, isn't it?" Molly turned towards the others, seemingly impervious to the awkward silence and icy glares thrown towards her.

I picked up the bits of glass and placed them on the table. "A bit slippery, that glass. I'm sure motherhood will be the making of her. Now, what plans have we for next week? Deborah, you first."

The rest of our time together was a blur and it was only when I saw the hills in front of me, it registered that I was back in Malvern. The sloping beauty of the hills invariably gave me a lift, but today I felt I was tumbling down an everlasting slope. Yes, I knew Jason had used me to get at my family for whatever weird and despicable reason, but now he had cheated on me with Margaret Schultz, no less. First Brendan, who, though he hadn't cheated on me had hidden things, and now Jason. It had all started all those years ago when as a child I had been abducted by one of the Davieses – Dan Davies – who was supposedly one of Emily's friends. Could I ever trust any man? Uncle Matt, of course. Colin Walker? Wonderful though he was, he had only employed me because I reminded him of his dead daughter.

What was it about me that made me such an easy target?

I couldn't help wondering whether when Margaret Schultz had welcomed Jason into her bed they had laughed together at the way they had treated me so contemptuously. Furthermore, did she know about the Jason-Beverley lies? Had she helped dream it up? I couldn't talk to Uncle Matt, Emily or even Beverley about it; I felt so belittled, so worthless. Bev, I never kept any secrets from, but this was a bridge too far.

A few days later when I met up with Deborah, I blurted out the question that must have nestled itself at the back of my mind. "Does Jason know about the baby?"

Deborah shifted uncomfortably in her seat as though she had a splinter in her bottom.

"I don't know," she answered finally.

I said nothing as the silence loomed between us and I watched her fidget once more. "But she wanted me to ask you something."

I slammed my coffee down on the table. "Really! That evil bitch wanted you to ask ME something? She's got a nerve."

"If you don't want me to I won't," Deborah murmured.

I slowly breathed out. "No, ignore my bad temper. You're piggy in the middle and I shouldn't take it out on you. What does that…what does Schultz want?"

"She wants to know how she can get in touch with Jason."

Of course that's what she wanted to know. Don't we all?

Jason, Schultz, baby. That nightmare was never far from my mind over the next few weeks. One afternoon as soon as work was over, I set out to walk. It was hammering down with rain, but what the hell, I needed fresh air to wash away all the evil thoughts that were flooding my head. I also needed wine to make sure they stayed away. I entered the shop, picked up the bottle nearest my hand and wandered to the desk where a head appeared from below the counter.

I gasped. "You!" I snarled before crashing the bottle down on the counter, turning and hurrying towards the door.

"Wait! Please! I have to ask you something. Please, Paula."

I stopped in my tracks. I'd never heard Schultz utter the word 'please' to anyone before.

"What would you want to know from me? All we have in common is – Jason Brown, apparently." The contempt came gushing out. "And I don't want to waste my time talking about that lowlife cheating shit."

"I'll lock up then we can go into the back room." She moved swiftly towards the door.

I hovered before slowly following her into a small lounge room.

"Please," she said, indicating the sofa.

I reluctantly sat, sitting upright as I gazed at the pregnant girl opposite.

She started. "I'm illegitimate. My father ran off before I was born and I've never met him or know anything about him. My mother never got over being left to bring me up by herself. Because of that, I was treated as a burden, a pain in the ass rather than a daughter to be loved and cherished." Her expression was hard and cold as she gazed at the wall behind me.

"That's sad, but what has that to do with me?"

"I need your help." Her eyes had an imploring look. "I have to find Jason and tell him about the baby."

I stood up. "I don't need to hear this."

"Paula, please don't go! It was a one-night stand. It meant nothing. Please stay."

I turned back and stared tight-lipped as she continued.

"He hadn't seen you for a couple of weeks. He thought you had finished with him so he turned up at the pub one night. We both had too much to drink and one thing led to another. This is the result." She looked down at her stomach, which was only slightly larger than normal. "You may not believe it, but he's the first person I've slept with since Clive and I split up ten months ago."

"So?"

"I have to get in touch with Jason to tell him about the baby, simply so the baby gets to know his father. Jason and I will never get together – ever – but the child should know him."

"So, you want an address or telephone number?"

"Yes, d'you…?"

"I don't have either. I wish I did."

I watched her face crumble. "Really, you have no way of getting in touch?"

She turned her back, but I could hear her sobbing.

"Margaret, I'm not lying – he's obviously ditched his old phone and got a new number. He doesn't want to be contacted because of stuff he did to me and my family."

"But I thought he was your boyfriend?" Her eyes were red and swollen.

I didn't want to go there; the subject was too painful. "If anything changes, I promise I'll let you know – promise."

I was shocked at how vulnerable she looked. "Paula, I'm sorry about everything. Please keep in touch."

I nodded, moved towards the door, before turning back. "Margaret, why were you so nasty to me? What did I do to you?"

She sighed. "I was wrong, but I had nothing. I couldn't stay on at school because I had to bring some money in by helping out here. Then I had to go to evening classes to get some sort of qualifications before landing a job at Walkers."

"So, what's that got to do with me?"

"You came from a privileged background with money. Your uncle got you your job, and let's just say you were Colin's favourite."

I glared angrily at her. "You know nothing about my background or how I got my job, so you made my life hell based on shit."

I slammed the door shut and strode out of the shop with my head down deep in thought. I needed some sort of change, some sort of different focus in my life. As much as I loved Uncle Matt, Emily, my sister and Harry, whenever I saw them now, I saw a dark cloud hovering over them. In the cloud were the Davieses peering down and laughing evil, brittle laughs. At work, as hard as I tried to be professional and businesslike, Deborah's weak smile brought Margaret Schultz and Jason into my mind no matter how hard I tried to push them aside.

I needed a new outlet and new friends, so I renewed my interest in the local netball club where I had been a member for some time but rarely visited. But then came the telephone call that shattered any semblance of peace that I'd manufactured.

"Paula, it's Beverley – your sister. D'you remember me?"

I managed a laugh, but my sister's tone became serious. "Paula, I've found him. I know where he is."

Chapter 44

Matt

I felt an arm reach around me and pull me to them – lips kissed my cheek.

"Darling, you must stop worrying – it's doing you no good at all."

"I know, I know."

"And Newman did threaten to call the police if you bothered him again."

"Yes, dear. It's the 'I was told to' that bothers me. I have to find out who's behind it all."

Emily's gentle expression eased some of the tension. "I think you know who's responsible for the whole shebang. I think Paula summed it up the other day when she said the object of the article and reviews was to cause the utmost pain and misery."

I pursed my lips and was just about to reply when Emily interrupted.

"Just like the Jason, Bev and Paula fiasco."

"Emily, come here." She folded into my arms as we stood like a couple of young lovers. "They are always there haunting us, but who and why now? We know it's the Davieses, but Gordon is no more, Dan is in Cyprus, so is it Tracy's illegitimate son and is that Jason Brown?"

I felt Emily's hand caress my bottom affectionately. "There is another question."

"What's that?"

"Whoever is behind it all, are they going to stop there, and if the answer to that is no, what is the next move. Is the whole thing going to escalate?"

Chapter 45

Beverley

I couldn't bear what Jason Davies or whoever he was, had done to my family. I had to do something. Paula was a wreck and had pushed us all to one side, and Uncle Matt had this haunted air which no matter how hard he tried to hide it, enveloped him and produced dark clouds under his eyes.

These worries were occupying my thoughts as I sat in the pub awaiting my friend Carolyn for a lunchtime get-together. I became aware of a smart-suited young man staring across at me, but I turned away quickly as Carolyn appeared. My ex-classmate and I had an amiable time updating each other on what we'd been up to, when my friend turned to me. "That guy over there keeps staring at you. D'you know him?"

"Yes, Jason and I had a meeting with him a few weeks ago to discuss a new website his company wanted. It wasn't the best. The way he looked at me it was quite obvious what he wanted apart from a website."

As I walked home, the idea hit me! Could I pull it off? There was only one way to find out.

An hour later I appeared at the reception of Ideal Services Ltd.

"Is Mr Carver available, please?" I put on my best business expression.

"Do you have an appointment?" she asked.

"I'm afraid not."

The serious face considered me then picked up the phone. "There's a…?"

"Just say it's Beverley."

Adam appeared immediately, looking hesitantly at me.

"Adam," I smiled. "I felt I must come and say hello after not being able to do so earlier. I was tied up in a networking lunch – new opportunity, you know. A man in your position is only too aware how important those are to small independents like myself. I wouldn't want you to think I was ignoring you."

I watched Adam relax and I breathed in, throwing out my chest.

"I really enjoyed the work I did with Jason on your website."

"I'm pleased about that," Adam spoke at last. "I enjoyed the time we spent together."

I had to move this along. "I hope your new site is up and running now?" I asked.

"Yes, it's going well. D'you want to come into my office?" he asked, peering across at the receptionist, who couldn't hide the curiosity from her face as she looked over.

I smiled once more and followed him, trying desperately to hide the feeling of vulnerability. "D'you want a tea or coffee?" he asked.

"Thank you, no. I don't want to take up too much of your time. I know you are a busy man."

I sat opposite him and decided to take the initiative. "Part of my agreement with Jason was that he would pay me the final twenty-five per cent for the work I did for him, when your website was up and running."

"Seems reasonable," Adam responded.

"So, now I know it's up and running I can push him for it. D'you have any contact details for him since he moved?"

Adam looked uncertainly at me. "I'm not sure…"

143

I flashed my eyes and crossed my legs.

"Well, I suppose…don't tell anyone you got it from me." He opened his filing cabinet, scrawled something on a compliment slip before tearing the top off and handing it over to me.

I glanced quickly at it, before standing up. "Thank you. I dare not take up any more of your time."

"Beverley, perhaps we could get together – have a drink sometime? Is tomorrow good for you?"

"What a shame! I'm sorry, I can't tomorrow but I'd love to meet up. Perhaps you could give me your number."

I hurried out of the building clutching the two compliment slips. As I passed a recycle bin, I made sure I threw the right one away before pulling out my phone and dialling Paula.

Chapter 46

Matt

"Come on in." I looked at the excitement on the girls' faces. "You look like you've both won the lottery."

"We all have," said Paula. "It was Bev's doing and it's better than money. We thought we should share it with you."

"You'd better come into the lounge. Emily and Harry will want to hear what you have to say."

"It's about Jason," said Beverley. "So, not too much about the lies he told."

"Of course not."

We sat down. "We know where he is," said Paula. "Tell them, Bev."

I listened as Beverley told me how she encouraged the information out of a work colleague.

"Are you going to hire a 'hit man' or send the fuzz in?"

"Harry!" scolded Emily.

"Well, after the lies he told about his affair with Bev, he deserves everything he gets," said Harry.

"How do you know about...?" asked Beverley.

"How could I not know after all the shouting and screaming that went on?" answered Harry as he studied his phone.

"But Harry has raised a good point. What can we do? We can't get the police involved because there is no criminal offence, either concerning the article, reviews or the other stuff." I stared out of the window at the trees swaying in the wind.

"Perhaps a hit man is the best option – sort it out once and for all," suggested Beverley.

Harry held his hand up for a high five, and laughed.

"Beverley, behave yourself. You're supposed to set an example," said Emily, trying hard to hide a grin.

I ignored the levity. "But what will they do next? They won't stop until they inflict the maximum pain, that's clear. It all started years ago before you lot came on the scene. They tried to get Emily booted out of her teaching job in disgrace by threatening the father of one her pupils. Then they bribed a fellow jogger to seduce me." I smiled at my wife. "That was never going to work – I loved Em far too much to risk losing her."

It went quiet as Emily reached over, took my hand and kissed it.

"But there's nothing to say they won't resort to violence if they don't manage to inflict enough emotional pain," I continued.

"Somehow, we need to take the initiative," said Paula, slowly and thoughtfully. "How, is the million-dollar question."

"At least we know where Jason is now," added Emily. "That's a start."

The following week, Paula laid the foundation for a possible way forward.

Chapter 47

Paula

I was absentmindedly tapping into the internet the address I knew off by heart, bringing up a map of the area where Jason lived, when the doorbell rang. It was Angela Moore.

"I was just passing, so I thought I'd call in and say hello."

I gave a wry smile.

"I know, I know – it happens to be true on this occasion."

I laughed at the earnest expression. "Come in – you're most welcome." I found I actually meant it, which was somewhat different from when she had first appeared at my door.

She settled into the lounge as I disappeared into the kitchen before handing over a coffee she hadn't asked for. "You don't know Bridgwater, do you?" I asked.

"No, I don't. Why, you're not moving, are you?"

I studied the concerned frown. "No, I'm not moving."

She breathed out. "Thank goodness for that. Brendan would be heartbroken."

"Angela, I know you mean well, but I'm not ready yet. I need time – there's too much going on."

"I understand that. When you say there's too much going on, is this to do with your question about Bridgwater?" she asked.

"Well, sort of. I'm thinking of going down there for a few days and need somewhere to stay, ideally near a particular address."

"I see." I saw the look of distrust flick across her face as she paused, waiting for an explanation.

Should I, I wondered? I took a drink of my coffee to buy time and peered over the cup, watching as Angela considered.

"I have a friend who works at an estate agent who could contact their Bridgwater branch? If you want me to?" she asked.

My eyes were fixed on the magnolia-coloured kitchen walls as I reflected once more on how gullible I had been. Jason had used me. He had had no feelings for me and my heart had not put up shutters, had sent no warning signals. That magical evening when he had bought theatre tickets for *Les Misérables* was a lie. Everything about him was a lie.

"Paula, are you all right? I said how did you swing this?" I watched as Uncle Matt spread his hands out to encompass the room and more.

"What? Oh, how did I find out about this place?" I gave a nervous laugh. "It was Angela."

Beverley sneered. "Not the whore?"

"Sis, I keep telling you she's all right, she's kosher."

"Now, now, you two, remember you're not two spoilt children any more. So, what did this Angela do, then?" Uncle Matt inquired.

"She has a friend who works at an estate agent and this friend contacted their fellow branch down here. This place has been up for rental for a few months and has had no offers, so I asked if we could have it for a fortnight, and here we are. Where we go from here though, I haven't a clue."

Uncle Matt grinned. "I think we'll just be friendly near neighbours. After all, Jason is across the road and not far from here, so we can keep an eye on him. But," he continued as the grin disappeared, "we will be on the front foot instead of waiting for them to make the next move."

We woke early the next morning, hurried downstairs and peered out of the window, waiting for movement. It was an hour later when Jason's door opened and out he stepped. I hurried out and darted down the street.

"Hi, Jason," I said in as relaxed a tone as I could muster.

He whirled round, eyes wide in alarm. "YOU, what are you doing here?"

"Oh, just spending time here, having a break. Are you okay?"

Jason stood transfixed, then looked back, unsure whether to return or not.

"Is Steve all right?" I asked innocently.

It was as if someone had smacked him in the face. "Steve? Steve, did you say? What d'you know about Steve?" He bent to pick up the briefcase that he had dropped to the floor.

"I'm just inquiring if he is okay, that's all."

"I said, what are you doing here?" he blustered.

"I told you, we are just having a bit of a relaxing break."

"We, who's we? Who else is here?"

"Just Beverley, Uncle Matt and me. We're just in that house down the road, number 7?"

"What! I've got no time to talk, I'm in a hurry."

I watched as he rushed towards his car. His phone was pushed to his ear as he drove off, mouthing furiously. I breathed a sigh of relief as I raced back to our house, tears threatening as I slumped into a chair.

"What happened?" cried Beverley and Uncle Matt in unison. I heard the words but they sounded a million miles away as I sat as if in a trance picturing that face.

"Sis, are you all right?" I looked down at the hand that gently stroked my arm.

I shook my head. "I wanted to scream and shout and hurl every obscenity I could think of at him. But I didn't – I couldn't. I had to do what we agreed. Be nice. Put him on the back foot, and that's what I did. But it was hard Bev. It was so hard."

"We are so proud of you, Paula, believe me. Now we wait and see what they do," said Uncle Matt with determination.

Chapter 48

Jason

"I need to see you straight away," I shouted down the phone, but nothing. Ten minutes later I tried again. "For Christ's sake, ring me back."

The hours went by and no answer, no matter how many times I rang.

By early evening I could not sit still, my emotions were running wild. Why were they here? What were they planning? I tried to distract myself by turning on the television but saw nothing.

Finally, I heard a knock on the door and there stood Steve.

I couldn't stop myself. "Where the hell have you been, and why didn't you answer my calls?" I shouted.

"I've been out all day and I forgot my phone. What's going on? Why are you so wound up?"

He followed me into the kitchen where I poured two large whiskies, spilling some as I handed one over. "It's number 7 across the road. The rental house they can never find tenants for?"

The doorbell rang and I nearly dropped my drink as I shuddered at the invasive sound. Steve looked at me before moving his head in the direction of the door. I opened it and gasped as I took in the smiling open face of Matt Bishop.

"I just wanted to say hello and see if you wanted to come over for a drink, but I see you've got one. Oh, hello, Steve, I don't think we've met before." I watched open-mouthed as he held out his hand towards my friend as he came towards the door. Steve kicked at the door, slamming it shut.

"What the hell's going on? What's he doing here and how the bloody hell did that bugger find us?"

The calm manner that I was used to was no more. His eyes were wide and he looked in a state of shock.

"That's why I've spent all day trying to contact you – to tell you they're here, on this street. What their plan is, I've no idea." I was pacing up and down as I spoke, but couldn't stop myself. "Where are you with the next round of plans?"

"I'm still trying to find someone to come on board with us. I've offered the usual, but no one seems keen."

He ignored me. "We need to ramp things up. They're here for a reason, and that can only mean one thing. We have to bring things to a head, and soon."

"How? What did you have in mind?"

Steve gave a wry smile that never reached his eyes. "I'll sleep on it, and see you tomorrow."

I opened the door to let him out.

"Oh, hi, Steve. Good to meet you – I'm Paula, but then I'm sure Jason has mentioned me."

I pushed the door shut, but that didn't stop Steve's avalanche of four-letter words hammering against my ears.

At eight o'clock the following morning Steve appeared once more. He was dishevelled and his eyes had a dark, haunted look. Before I could say anything, he held up his hand. "Our plans haven't worked. What we wanted to do was to mutilate, humiliate and ruin the Bishop family for the way they ruined and ultimately murdered our guardian and mentor. Gordon would still be with us but for those evil people. We tried to drive an irreparable wedge between those two whores, but they're here together, so that didn't work. We thought Matt Bishop would be lost when his professional reputation was in tatters, but he appeared at your door with an infuriating smile. Subtlety is dead. We need to do more."

I turned away from Steve as a note was pushed through the letterbox. "What did you have in mind?"

The writing didn't resonate with me. I read and gasped; it was from Matt Bishop.

"I don't know, but we need to be more ruthless," continued Steve, unaware of the note that would spark even more hysteria.

> *Dear Jason,*
>
> *Delighted that we are now neighbours.*
> *Paula, Beverley and I would love to get together with you and Steve for dinner, and a few drinks for a fun evening when it is convenient.*

Steve stopped what he was saying as he saw my expression and snatched the note from my hand. He read it, before tearing it up and throwing it in the air.

His face was bright red, his eyes wide and wild as he marched down the garden towards the shed before reappearing carrying a sledgehammer.

"Steve, don't!" I cried.

"They're treating us like fools. They're waving two fingers at us!"

Chapter 49

Paula

"They're both there, are they?" asked Uncle Matt.

"I guess. Both their cars are outside. What d'you think the chances are, of getting a reply, I mean?"

Uncle Matt shrugged. "Who knows?"

"And if they say 'yes', do we really have to feed them?" asked Beverley, as she turned to me grimacing. "Can you cook cow dung? Um, perhaps you can in a pie," she mused.

A loud crunching noise broke into our reverie, the sound crashing through the open windows and battering the eardrums.

"What the...?" Uncle Matt raced out, the crunching sound of metal upon metal sickening as the door was opened.

"STOP IT!" shouted Matt as the sledgehammer was brought down crashing against his car windscreen, sending glass flying. The large, intimidating hammer was pulled back as Matt pushed against Steve, knocking him off balance.

"I SAID STOP!" His car was a mess, the bonnet a mutilated corpse full of large dents, any resemblance to its original shape a distant memory. Manic eyes glared towards the man who had pushed him and with a powerful punch knocked Matt to the ground.

The sledgehammer was pulled back once more and smashed into the passenger door.

"ENOUGH!" cried Matt as he attempted to lift himself off the ground.

Steve turned towards him and raised the hammer high into the air.

"NO!" I screamed, before hiding my face in my hands, unable to view the horror that was unfolding. When I took them away, I had to shake my head, uncertain of what I was seeing. Steve was on the ground unconscious with a man looming over him rubbing his hand.

I brushed tears away from my eyes. "Brendan? Is it really you?"

He nodded, still rubbing his hand.

Jason appeared, his face deathly pale. "I tried to stop him, I did really. He just wouldn't listen." He reached down and picked up the sledgehammer as Steve slowly came round.

"Why are you here? How did you know we were here? Did you know he was going to smash the car up?" There was so much I wanted to know.

"Hang on, don't you mean 'How lovely to see you, Brendan'? Is that what you meant to say?"

"Of course it's lovely to see you." I moved towards him and folded myself into his body before kissing him.

"Perhaps you could leave that for a moment." I turned to see Beverley bending down to help Uncle Matt to his feet. "I've called the police. They'll be here in a minute."

Steve got up groggily. "Did someone mention police?"

"What the hell d'you expect – look what you've done." Beverley waved a finger at the car.

"And what you would have done if Brendan hadn't stopped you?" I added.

"I wasn't going to do anything. I was just waving the hammer about, that's all."

The sound of the police car invaded the space, until it ground to a halt.

Uncle Matt, Jason and Steve climbed into the car and off they went to the police station.

"So, what brought you here? How did you know what was going on?" Beverley was upstairs and Brendan and I sat snuggled on the sofa with a glass of wine.

"It was Angela." He paused. "My half-sister. I'll repeat, my half-sister. She told me about the conversation you had about staying in Bridgwater and I put two and two together. I was just worried for you, that's all."

I kissed him. "I'm glad you were. I shudder to think what might have happened but for you." I shook my head, my vision blurring at the image of the sledgehammer being drawn back and pointed towards Uncle Matt.

Chapter 50

Emily

The phone rang and I rushed towards it, expecting it to be Matt, but it was a woman.

"Emily?"

I recognised the voice but couldn't place it.

"It's Liz, Liz Davies."

"Oh, Liz, how are you?" I cursed my stupidity. Her husband had died only a month ago and I had asked how she was.

"Oh, not too bad, but I've just got back from Cyprus and picked up a couple of answerphone messages from you. You sounded rather concerned?"

"Liz, don't worry – we've sorted things out, but it's very good of you to phone."

"Is it to do with Jason?"

I hesitated.

"It is, isn't it? He's been causing trouble with your family again, hasn't he?"

I felt a lump in my throat. I could still picture the young bright-eyed friend from my teaching days at St Michaels when everything seemed simple and straightforward. "Liz, I don't want to cause any trouble for you. You've had enough problems and sadness to contend with. I don't want to make things worse."

"Tell me everything, Emily. Don't hold back. Gordon helped to put Jason and Steve back on track and he was desperate for them to follow the right path."

There was no point in trying to fob her off. I took a deep breath. "You know that Paula and Jason were an item?" I started.

"Oh, were they? What, your Paula and Jason?" she said hesitantly.

"Yes, our Paula. I see, if you didn't know about that you wouldn't know about his fabricated affair with Beverley?"

"No!"

"Or the lies he got someone to post online about Matt's business dealings?"

"No," she sighed, "I didn't know any of this."

We talked for some time before Liz acknowledged that she would have to have a serious word with both of them before things escalated to the point of no return.

"Gordon feared that his death might lead them back into their bad ways. He left a note for them. Anyway, leave it with me and I'm sorry for all the bad things they've done to you and your family."

"Liz, it's not your..."

"I'll be in touch. Bye, Emily."

I put the phone down and stared out into the garden where Matt and I had spent many happy hours working or just lounging. Now all I could see was darkness, clouds and shadows. I shouldn't have let them go – how could I have been so stupid? I felt fear coursing through my body. Everything that was precious to me was at serious risk. I rang Matt's mobile. 'It rang and rang.' No answer. I couldn't help it – the tears began to flow.

Chapter 51

Beverley

I'd left Paula and Brendan alone so they could sort things out. I was wrong: clearly they were an item and Brendan was not the monster I thought he was. I was busy absentmindedly doodling when I heard the doorbell. "I'll get it," I shouted and raced downstairs.

"Oh, hello." The woman in front of me was well dressed but wore a worried frown.

"I'm sorry to bother you." She screwed up her face. "It's Beverley, isn't it?"

"Ye-s." Who was this lady?

"I'm looking for Jason Brown who's at number 10 across the street, but he doesn't appear to be in. I wondered if you had any idea?"

"Mm, I'm not sure."

"I'm Liz Davies, an old friend of your mum, Emily. I spoke to her earlier today, she said you were at this address."

I couldn't help but shudder at the name 'Davies'. I paused as I tried to regroup. But despite that I could see that she was on edge. "You'd better come in."

Paula and Brendan wandered over, intrigued by the unknown voice. "You're Paula, aren't you?"

"Yes, and you're Liz Potter, Aunt Emily's old work friend. It's a long time since we last met." I could see Paula put on her best friendly face.

"I'm trying to find Jason. I spoke to Emily earlier and I'm concerned that things might unravel."

"Sit down, Liz, and I'll tell you what happened."

Liz slumped down into the chair, a tell-tale look of foreboding etched across her face.

Paula's phone started to ring. "Hi, Emily, can I ring you back? I've got your old friend Liz Potter here. Hold on, I'll pass you on to Bev." She handed me the phone and whispered, "She wants to know what's going on. She's being trying to reach Uncle Matt. She's beside herself."

"Where's Matt? I've been trying to ring him for the last two hours but his phone is switched off."

I tried to think of a way to dress it up but couldn't. "He's at the police station."

"What? Is he…?"

"He's fine, Emily."

"Tell me what's going on, I want to know everything."

I told her. "So, that's what Steve did – he smashed up the car. But thanks to Brendan…yes, he's here. Thanks to him, no one got hurt." I listened to Emily as she poured out her emotions, and I tried to reassure her. "You can trust Liz" were her final words before I disconnected.

Liz had been listening in. "So, Steve is at the police station along with Jason and your Matt?"

Paula nodded.

"Then I need to be there." She moved towards the door.

Paula grabbed her coat. "I'll come with you."

Liz turned. "You can trust me."

I smiled at Paula. "That's what Emily said."

Chapter 52

Paula

I'd never had reason to set foot in a police station before. The people dressed in uniforms seemed stern and the walls seem to close in on me. I felt the entrance door slam shut behind me as I approached the reception desk. Tired eyes turn upwards towards Liz and me.

"Yes?" he offered.

"I understand Steve, Steven Collins is here?" Liz asked.

"Yes, that's right," Tired Eyes answered.

"Could I see him?"

I watched as the receptionist policeman studied the smartly dressed woman next to me as he considered.

"Are you his mother?" he inquired.

"No," Liz hesitated. "Not exactly. I'm his mother's sister-in-law."

The policeman frowned.

"His mother lives in Cyprus."

He studied the papers in front of him, before nodding off to his right. "Room 4a. I'd better take you there."

We hurried after the policeman to the room and entered. There stood Jason and Steve engaged in a heated conversation which ceased immediately. Steve's gaze fixed on Liz while I found Jason's bright eyes locked onto mine before he turned away, clearly embarrassed.

Before anyone could speak, the door opened and in walked another officer.

160

"Who are you two?" he asked as his eyes scanned Liz and me.

Liz turned towards him completely unfazed. "As I explained to this policeman here."

"She said she's related to this young man's mother who lives in Cyprus"

"Yes, and I'd like to know…"

"Thanks Ted." The receptionist policeman left the room. "Let's all take a seat, shall we?" He took a pen out of his top pocket. "Right then."

"Why are Steven and Jason here, officer?" Liz asked.

The officer, who it transpired was Sergeant Penfold, wrinkled his forehead in confusion. "Because this young man" – he looked down at the papers in front of him – "Steven Collins, smashed up Mr Bishop's car with a sledgehammer."

"But that's what he was instructed to do by Emily Bishop. Let me explain, as it's clear you haven't given Steven an opportunity to do so as yet."

I marvelled at the calm and composed way in which Liz Potter had assumed control, though where Aunt Emily fitted into this I hadn't a clue.

"Mr Bishop's car is about fifteen years old and he is very attached to it as he has every right to be. Except this year," she sighed, "the steering became dodgy and the brakes very definitely not good."

"I see," sneered Penfold. "So, what has that to do with Collins taking a sledgehammer to it?"

"Emily was desperate for him to get rid of it as it was so unsafe, but he wouldn't. So she voiced her concerns to Jason, who told me about the problem as I have connections to a motor dealer."

I watched as Sergeant Penfold pushed his pad away as he tried to take this in. "Slow down. Emily is?"

161

"Emily is Matt Bishop's wife."

"And how is he" – he pointed his finger at Jason – "connected to Emily?"

"He was my boyfriend at the time," I interrupted.

"I see, I think," said Penfold. "Very interesting, but once again, what has this to do with Collins smashing up Bishop's car?"

Liz continued. "Jason had become very fond of Paula's parents so when he split with her, he was keen to do something to show his affection for them."

"Ye-s?"

"So, he has paid for a similar car only a couple of years old, which Gordon Davies Motors have sorted for me."

"I see, but you still haven't told me where Collins and the sledgehammer come into this…this story?" He glanced at his pad again. "Mrs Davies."

"The only way to ensure that Matt Bishop would agree to take ownership of this new car is if his old beloved car was written off, and that's what Steven did. It had next to no value anyway, believe me."

Penfold raised his eyebrows towards Jason and Steve, who nodded vigorously. I felt stunned and confused, how could she come out with such nonsense? "Sergeant that's rubbish."

"That's what I said Paula, the car is rubbish, it has no value." Liz gaze me a hard look.

"Right, I want you all out of here." Penfold waved his hands. "Back to the waiting room."

He got up and followed them out, then beckoned to Uncle Matt. "Mr Bishop, come with me."

Chapter 53

Matt

I followed the uniform into the stark, pale room and sat opposite him as instructed. A sympathetic smile creased his face, but rather than reassure me, it made me uncertain.

"Did you know Collins was going to smash your car up?"

I lurched back in my chair. "Is that a serious question? Have you dragged me in here to ask me that?

Sergeant Penfold ignored the response as he flipped over the pages in front of him. "So, this car – how long have you had it?"

"About twelve years."

"And how roadworthy is it?"

I gave a wry grin. "Do you mean now, or before the sledgehammer?"

Penfold gave me an icy glare.

"Okay, it wasn't perfect. It needed some work on it, which I've got booked in with my usual service guy. I know – or should I say, knew – I needed to change it, but it has sentimental value. My wife and the girls kept on at me to get rid of it but I kept putting it off. Now I've got no choice."

Penfold put down his pen and gave me a hard stare. "What's your take on why Collins did what he did?"

I shrugged.

He paused and looked down at his notes. "You're on holiday, aren't you, and staying on the same street as Jason Brown?"

"That's right – been here two days."

"Why so close?"

"Why not? A friend of Paula recommended it."

He thought once more. "No falling out since you've been here?"

"No, I've asked him and Steve Collins round for a drink, but that hasn't happened yet."

Sergeant Penfold sighed, already bored with the questioning. "What if I tell you that he was simply doing what he was asked to do?"

"What? Are you serious? Who asked him? This is ridiculous?" I stood up.

"Sit back down and listen."

I sat and listened as he told me how Emily, the girls and Liz Potter had coerced Jason and Steve Collins into writing off my beloved car as a means of safeguarding my existence. I listened, my mouth open as he rambled on. Finally, he stood up and opened the door. "Come with me."

We went back to the waiting room where the other worried faces sat.

"Right," said Penfold as he puffed out his chest. "You lot have wasted enough police time. In future, try talking to one another instead of bothering us. Now, clear off and don't come back."

We left.

As we approached Liz's car, Paula gave me an imploring look, her eyes resting on Steve's back as he walked ahead, talking to Jason. "What happened?"

"We'll talk about it later?" I replied.

"But?"

"Later, please, Paula." I tried to smile but failed.

It was a quiet journey back to our houses. After parking up, Liz turned to Jason and Steve. "I think we all need to get together tomorrow morning and sort out one or two things. Your place at eleven o'clock Jason." It was not a question.

They grunted before shuffling away.

"Thanks for trusting me, Matt." She attempted a smile but it was a stretch too far.

"Well, thank you for contacting Emily and telling her what you were going to say to the police. Just as well I turned my phone on eventually."

Liz drove off, leaving Paula and me gazing at the broken glass in the gutter leading to our house. We had moved here to try and take the bull by the horns and force the Davieses' hand and it had worked – it had certainly worked. But now we were too shell-shocked to draw any satisfaction from it. My head could still picture the manic glare of Collins as he drew the sledgehammer back, ready to smash it into me. If it hadn't been for Brendan I would be debris along with the broken glass in the gutter.

As soon as we were inside, Paula turned to me. "Why isn't Collins in jail?"

It was a fair question. Why wasn't he? "Because Emily phoned me and told me what Liz Potter planned to say and that I should trust her and confirm her story. Don't ask me why, but Emily wouldn't say such a thing without good reason."

"I know," sighed Paula, "but it seems strange after getting them, or Collins at least, in police custody. It was the perfect result for us, then we concoct a story to get them off. Why?"

I sighed. "We'll find out tomorrow at 11am. All will be revealed."

Beverley and Brendan appeared. "What happened?" asked Bev, almost rubbing her hands with excitement.

So, I told her.

"But that's all bullshit! Why would you confirm such a pile of crap after what happened?"

"Emily said…"

"You told me what Emily said, but it doesn't make sense. Gordon Davies and Liz Potter or Davies, were like second parents

165

to those two tossers, so Liz is bound to do anything she can to get them off." I watched Beverley move around as she sought to control her anger as she flung out the angry words.

"Please, Bev. I can understand why you are upset, but try and contain it and listen to what Liz has to say tomorrow morning."

Beverley stormed off.

Chapter 54

Paula

Breakfast was a strangely quiet affair. No one wanted to mention the events of yesterday or indeed, the meeting later that morning. Beverley's usual lively expression was missing as she tapped away at her mobile phone. Brendan looked across at me and smiled. It was a warm smile that for one brief moment brought a comforting glow into the room and took away the apprehension for the day ahead. Uncle Matt was constantly looking down at his watch. The tap at the door shattered the silence.

"Whenever you're ready?" came the voice of Liz Potter. "I'm sorry, I know it's early but I thought..."

"That's fine – we'll be there in a few minutes," Uncle Matt replied before coming back into the dining room to pass on the message.

"Don't bother," said Beverley, "we heard."

We walked along and across the road, each of us locked in our own private world, before entering Jason's house. We settled into the seats offered us. Steve Collins tried to ignore us, a defiant glint in his eyes. And though Jason attempted to adopt a friendly smile, the lies he had concocted erected an insurmountable barrier that would never go away.

Liz appeared with a warm, relaxed expression that tried but failed to hide her nervousness.

"Thanks for coming round this morning and for confirming the story I told yesterday. I hope God will forgive me for all the lies I came out with." I was distracted by her hands, which she kept rubbing together.

"Before dear Gordon passed away, he wrote me a letter which he said I could read after he was gone. Well, I could only bring myself to open it when I was away in Cyprus and part of it relates to you two." She fixed her gaze on Jason and Steve.

"I'll read it and please listen carefully to what he was desperate for you to hear. He said:

> *In my early years I was a bad person. Greedy, arrogant and controlling, all because I had an important position in Davies Motors, which I hadn't earned, by the way. I thought that whatever I wanted I should have and woe betide anyone who got in the way. My time in prison was totally deserved and not a day goes by without me shuddering at the thought of what might have been but for the arrival of the police. But my incarceration opened up a whole new world that I had never seen or envisaged before. Through it I found God and found my dearest, darling Liz. Since the start of what I think of as my proper life, I have had more happiness than most people experience in twice as many years as I have been lucky to enjoy.*
>
> *Jason and Steve both had a difficult start to their lives, but they must understand that I rejoice at the life I have had. They believe wrongly that Matt and Emily Bishop were responsible for my lost years and that somehow that caused my condition, my Parkinson's. They don't understand – I have had a wonderful life!*
>
> *I know the two of them have been scheming to bring unhappiness to the Bishop family as some sort*

of retribution, but it is wrong, so very wrong, and it has to stop.

As you know, I still have shares in Davies Motors and in my will I have passed those shares equally to Jason and Steve with one proviso. If you, darling Liz, judge that either of them have behaved badly towards any of the Bishops then their ownership of the shares will be cancelled and they will be returned to you. I know you will be a fair and impartial judge even though you love them dearly."

Liz Potter turned towards the two stunned beneficiaries. "What d'you think?"

I watched as they looked at one another, neither of them able to speak. The ringing of a phone broke into the tension and Uncle Matt delved into his pocket, before disappearing into the hallway out of earshot.

"It's Emily. She's outside. She asked if it's okay to come in?"

"Perfect timing," said Liz, her eyes lighting up for the first time that day as she moved towards the door to welcome her. Emily came into the room and gave Matt a kiss and Beverley and me a warm hug before gushing out. "It's brilliant, much better than the old one. It turned up at eight o'clock this morning. I was barely out of bed. Thanks so much to you both." She studied the confused expressions of Jason and Steve. "Of course, you haven't seen it. Come and have a look."

"Go on," encouraged Liz.

Uncle Matt, Emily, Beverley, Brendan and I followed Jason and Steve as they traipsed down the road and stood before the nearly new, gleaming white Golf GTI. Uncle Matt climbed into the driver's seat and studied the interior with a satisfied smile.

Jason uttered the words we were all thinking. "It's very nice, Mrs Bishop, but why did you thank us?"

"Ah," said Liz. "Let's go back indoors."

They settled back into the dining room as Liz organised coffees and teas. Jason in particular looked extremely nervous. "Why did you thank Steve and me?"

"I can answer that," interrupted Liz. "Because the new car came from Davies Motors and you are both paying for it."

"What? That's impossible! I haven't got any money or even a job. That car must have cost at least fifteen thousand."

"Fifteen thousand five hundred to be precise."

"We haven't got that sort of money, Liz. It would take forever to pay it off, even if we got it on HP," said Jason.

"It's all sorted," said Liz. "I have spoken to Dan Davies, who is the major shareholder, and he is happy to offer you both jobs, starting in two weeks' time. Payment will come out of your wages over the next nine months."

"Working? At Davies Motors? You're kidding me?" Steve got up from his chair and began pacing up and down. "And if we refuse?"

"Steve, listen, think of that letter Liz read to us earlier. We need to make a fresh start and perhaps this is the opportunity we need. Liz has our best interests at heart – we know that," Jason urged.

Steve stared at his friend, his expression hardening. "We made a pact, don't you remember? We said nothing would stand in the way of ruining this garbage. Now some shares are offered to you and that promise means nothing. Friend," he sneered, "you're horse shit, you're nobody." He stormed out of the building, slamming the door shut.

Jason stared down at the floor. No one knew the right words to break the threatening silence that hovered over us. Finally, it was Uncle Matt who spoke. "Unless there's anything else, Liz, I think we'll make our way back to the house, then we can pack and return home."

"Off course. I'm sorry about Steve. When he's had a chance to think about what was said, he'll see things differently." Liz spoke quietly, trying to neutralise the tension that hung in the air.

We all stood and made our way to the door as first Emily then Uncle Matt hugged Liz as they left. No one was able to look at Jason.

After we had finished packing, Brendan and I waved the others off in the bright new car. I realised at that moment that there was something I just had to do. "Back in a minute, Brendan." I kissed him before marching down the street, where a morose Jason answered the doorbell.

"Sorry, Jason. I had to see you before we left," I gushed.

He moved aside to let me in. "It's important," I continued.

"I'll never forgive myself for what I did to you, Paula. I thought the world of you, I really did." I saw the hope in his eyes as he moved towards me.

I stepped back. "You're a lying, cheating, evil bastard, Jason Brown, but I didn't come here to tell you that." I watched his shoulders slump and uncertainty line his face. "D'you remember Margaret Schultz?" The red wave descended once more as he nodded.

"Well, here is her number. Ring her immediately."

He nodded once more.

"Promise me you will, Jason. We'll never be friends again after what you did, but if you honour that promise I'll think less badly of you."

"I promise," he muttered.

I couldn't resist it – I leaned forward and kissed him on the cheek. He looked at me, eyes wide in surprise as his hand went to his face.

"That's for helping bring Brendan and me get together again." I turned and left.

Chapter 55

Paula

The events of that day were erased from our conversation though not from our minds. We had imagined a feeling of relief and euphoria if we could fracture the way in which Jason and Steve infiltrated our lives. Instead, the words "we said nothing would stand in the way of ruining this garbage" hovered above us like a dark, grey cloud. We got on with living. Anything connected to the Davieses was off the menu, though Emily did make the occasional telephone call to Liz Potter.

Brendan and I moved in together and I often wondered how on earth I could have doubted his love for me. One evening he was out with his mates and I was preparing to leave to meet up with Beverley when my mobile rang.

"Yes?" I inquired, cursing the timing of the call.

"Paula?" I knew the voice but in my rush to leave I didn't bother to think who it was.

"Paula, I have to speak to you."

I felt icicles slide down my spine. "Jason, how dare you phone me?"

"I have to tell you."

"*NEVER PHONE ME AGAIN. I NEVER WANT TO SPEAK TO YOU, DON'T YOU KNOW THAT*?" I turned the phone off with shaking hands.

"You're late, Sis," said my sister as I arrived in The Bear and Ragged Staff half an hour later. "What's happened?" she asked, staring at my pale expression.

"It's Jason. He phoned just as I was coming out."

"No! What did he want?"

"I don't know and I don't care. I turned my phone off. Will they never go away, Sis?"

She passed me a double whisky. "Here, you look like you could use this. I suspect he wants to get back together with you."

I gave a dismissive laugh.

I watched Beverley with her chin in her hand, in deep thought.

"What are you thinking about?" I asked.

"Have you thought about changing your number?"

As usual, what my sister said made sense. The following day I changed my SIM card and passed my new number to those that I trusted. That list most definitely did not include the Davieses or anyone with the slightest connection to that dastardly lot.

Chapter 56

Paula

Brendan and I were laughing wildly, hand in hand as we walked back from town after a clothes-shopping expedition. My other hand carried the bag containing a top that Brendan insisted was perfect – right colours, right style, the price unimportant as it was made especially for me, so he said. The laughter ground to halt as we neared the couple in front.

"What is it?" asked Brendan.

I let go of his hand and rushed on. "Margaret, Jason, it *is* you."

They turned and gasped. "Paula!"

I looked down at the pram that Margaret was pushing and gave an instinctive smile as I gazed at the sleeping baby. "Oh, Margaret – she's beautiful."

"She is," grinned Jason. "Bella is the most beautiful baby ever – takes after her mother."

Brendan caught up. "Hi, both."

"Hi," they answered in unison.

"Why don't you come back with us?" asked Margaret. "We only live just around the corner. We've got a lot to catch up on."

I looked at Brendan and he nodded, albeit without any enthusiasm.

As we followed them back to their house, I shook my head. Why on earth did I accept an invitation for a social tête-à-tête with the two people who had caused such mayhem in my life over the last couple of years?

We entered the small cottage and Margaret said, "Jason will sort out teas, coffees and biscuits, while I put baby Bella to bed." She chuckled. "That's got a lovely ring to it, 'baby Bella to bed'."

As he passed me my coffee, Jason looked me in the eye. "I will never forgive myself for the way I treated you, Paula. The lies, the deceit. And I can never thank you enough for making me contact Maggie."

I looked away, not wanting to go down that route. "How long have you been here?"

"Here, in Malvern? About three months, I think. I tried to contact you and tell you what was going on, but I don't blame you for not wanting to speak to me."

Margaret entered the room and slumped down in the sofa. I noticed straight away that the guarded expression, downturned mouth and suspicious glare had gone and now there was a warm, radiant glow about her. She looked young and alive, a different person altogether.

I couldn't resist asking: "Was the birth difficult?"

Margaret smiled a contented smile. "I forgot the pain as soon as I saw her. It was the best day of my life – nothing will ever equal it."

Jason laughed. "It was painful for me watching but I coped, just."

"Thanks for making Jason contact me, Paula – it transformed my life," continued Margaret.

"That's okay. Jason said you'd only been here about three months, so is Bella a Bridgwaterite?"

"She is," grinned Margaret. "We should tell you what happened, shouldn't we, Jase? Shall I?"

"Go on, then."

I listened as she explained. "One day to my amazement, Jason phoned and said that you had insisted that he should call me. Why, he had no idea. So, I told him that I was travelling down that way and I would like to pop in and see him. He said okay, and we fixed a time. I didn't want to tell him about my pregnancy over the phone. I was desperate to see his reaction, and I wanted to be in control of the meeting. I couldn't risk him not turning up or cancelling at the last minute."

Jason sighed. "As if I'd do that."

"But when we met up and I told him, at first he went white and speechless and I thought, that's it, I'm out of here. Then, it was so funny. He looked at my belly, pulled me into his arms and said it was the happiest day of his life. He was ecstatic." She grabbed his hand. "Weren't you, gorgeous?"

"I was and still am and will be for ever."

It went quiet for what seemed ages as Brendan and I absorbed these words.

"So," asked Brendan finally, "did you stay down there, Margaret?"

"Yeah, I stayed while Jase was working at Davies Motors, which you didn't enjoy, did you?"

Jason shook his head.

"Then a couple of months later, as we were packing to come back here, things happened. My waters broke and Jase rushed me to hospital. He panicked while I tried to keep calm, honestly. Then Bella arrived." A huge smile spread across her face as she looked lovingly towards Jason.

We talked for some time before Margaret said, "Sorry, I must go and feed Bella."

"We must be going anyway," said Brendan, looking at his watch.

"Can I quickly say bye-bye to Bella? I will be quick, promise."

I went into the bedroom and ignored the double bed as I moved quietly towards the cot. I studied the beautiful face of baby Bella as her eyes opened wide as she looked at me and smiled.

The sweetness of that smile, the dimples and pudgy clenched fingers, reached into a part of me that I didn't know existed. The spell was broken as she started crying.

"She needs feeding," said Margaret, nervously pulling down her top.

I hurried out of the room, anxious to leave the mother alone to perform her most vital duty. Brendan smiled as I rejoined him, clearly relieved that he was no longer on a one-to-one with Jason. As we were about to leave, he stopped. "Are you still in touch with your mate Collins?"

The friendly smile disappeared from Jason's face. "I haven't seen or heard from him since that day in Bridgwater."

"He didn't work at Davies Motors, then?"

"No, he didn't."

Chapter 57

Brendan

When we arrived home, I assumed Paula would be desperate to share her views on the strange, friendly meet-up with her lying, cheating ex-boyfriend and vindictive work colleague, but she didn't. She seemed lost in a distant world.

"That was an afternoon we didn't expect, love," I ventured.

"We didn't."

I waited, expecting more, but nothing came. "Margaret didn't say anything to upset you, did she, when you went to see Bella?"

"Nothing like that – she was very kind. She's a different person from the one she used to be. Brendan, I need to talk to you." She reached out and took my hand. I could see from her earnest expression that this was serious. I tried to prepare myself for what was to come, but it was not what I expected. "Today I opened my eyes to a new world."

"Go on."

"My life up to now has been about me. My work, my relationships – it's all been about me. What with losing my birth parents at an early age, my grandparents unable to cope, then being abducted by the Davieses. All these things I think put me on the back foot. Perhaps I've been a bit guarded, a bit cautious?"

"I understand, Paula. You had it anything but easy. But where are you going with this? How can I help? And why now?"

I watched her eyes fill with tenderness. "I'm ready to move on to the next stage of my life, Brendan. Seeing baby Bella made me realise how desperately I want children. I want us to devote our lives to others, to our children."

I saw the love in her eyes and understood. Our children, she'd said – what a wonderful phrase. "I agree, one hundred per cent, two hundred per cent, a million per cent." I hugged her to me. "There's just one thing we need to do first."

She looked at me with uncertainty. "I know, but that's not a problem, is it? It hasn't been up to now."

"No, not that." I paused, waiting for the penny to drop.

Her eyes grew wide and her hand went to her mouth in surprise. "D'you mean what I think you mean?"

I smiled. "I do."

She folded herself into my arms. "That's my answer, darling, darling husband and father-to-be."

Chapter 58

Steve Collins

I'd left Bridgwater immediately after that fateful meeting with the Bishops and the two people in the whole world I thought I could trust and had proved me wrong. Liz, I could sort of understand – she was still reeling from the loss of Gordon, but Jason – never.

I sold the shares in Davies Motors that had been passed to me, settled my outstanding debt, and wandered around the country doing any sort of menial job I could to try and clear my confused mind.

Finally, I returned to Bridgwater and decided to confront Liz Davies. But of course, as soon as I clapped eyes on that gentle, Christian face, any less-than-charitable thoughts went out the window. We updated each other on what we had been up to, then she asked, "Have you been in contact with Jason?"

I shook my head.

"He's living with Margaret, Margaret Schultz. They have a baby daughter, Bella. He's very happy."

"Good."

"Oh, Steve – Jason's moved on and started a new life. You need to do the same. You're a good person – Gordon believed in you."

"No one could be a better person than Gordon, but a fat lot of good it did him." No matter how hard I tried, the pent-up anger bubbled to the surface.

She grasped hold of my hand. "Steve, please, remember Gordon's letter I read to you, and start a fresh life. He would almost beg you to."

I released her hand and studied my fingers.

Liz continued. "I spoke to Emily Bishop a couple of days ago. She tells me Paula is getting married on the fourteenth – that's Saturday week – to Brendan, of course, so everyone is settling down. You need to do the same."

We talked some more, but as we left, I had the start of a plan floating along the back of my mind. Liz had let slip the church and time of the service, and though she had been invited, had decided not to attend. That information was locked away and could not be forgotten.

I shaved off my long dark, flowing locks and let my facial hair grow. On the day of the wedding I put a pair of sunglasses in the pocket of my smart business suit as I drove off towards Malvern and the church. I waited, constantly looking at my watch before entering.

"Bride or groom?" inquired the usher.

"Groom," I replied with a smile, before moving into the aisle as instructed. I stared ahead, determined not to catch anyone's eye, then I became aware of the murmuring behind me.

"It is," I heard. "It's him, it's Steve."

Next, I heard a body pushing past others, with numerous "excuse me's", then the person who had been my closest friend and conspirator for many years, sat at my side.

"Steve, it *is* you. How are you? I've tried to contact you many times but you never answer."

I ignored him and continued to stare ahead.

"I didn't think you would be here." There was a pause then a sharp intake of breath. "Why are you here? Why the beard and bald look? God, what evil plan have you hatched up? Steve, don't, don't ruin their day."

I heard a 'shush' from the seat behind and Jason slid slowly away. I took a deep breath and put on my purest, most Christian expression as my eyes followed Brendan walking slowly down the aisle. Then a young woman sat next to me and offered me her hand. "I'm Angela, Brendan's half-sister." I felt compelled to accept the handshake and even though my mind was firmly fixed on my mission I couldn't help staring into the gentle face.

"You're Steve, aren't you? Jason has told me about you – what a good person you are. How you helped Gordon Davies and the less well-off in the local community. Don't ruin it, Steve. You have so much to give."

I stared ahead, wishing the service would hurry up. Where was the bride?

The voice was soft and gentle. "Don't do it, Steve. It will ruin your life, not theirs."

I could feel the sweat running down my back as Paula appeared to the murmuring of the congregation. It wouldn't be too long now before the vicar asked the question to which I would give an answer that Paula Bishop and Brendan Foster would remember for ever.

The bride handed over her flowers to Matt Bishop as the vicar began. As I watched, the words kept drumming into my brain: *She's a whore; slept with everyone – men and women. She's a bitch, an evil bitch!*

A soft hand reached over and took my hand in hers as she looked intently into my eyes.

The melodic tones began. "Dearly beloved, we are gathered together here in the sight of God – and in the face of this company – to join together this man and this woman in holy matrimony, which is commended to be honourable among all men; and therefore – is not by any – to be entered into unadvisedly or lightly – but reverently, discreetly, advisedly and solemnly." I gulped, preparing myself to stand up and shout:

I can, she's a whore; slept with everyone – men and women. She's a bitch, an evil bitch!

The vicar droned on, unaware of the mayhem that was about to unfold. "Into this holy estate these two persons present now come to be joined."

My hand was taken into the warm soft hands and squeezed. "Please, Steve, I beg you."

"If any person can show just cause why they may not be joined together – let them speak now or forever hold their peace."

I tried to move but my legs were like lead and my body stapled to the pew as the vicar continued.

"Thank you," mouthed Angela.

I remember nothing more of the service. I felt lifeless and lost as Angela took my arm and walked me out of the church. I had failed – I was useless and worthless. I wanted to run and leave this theatre behind but Angela clutched me and dragged me to the happy, laughing gathering that was posing for photos. They all had big wide soppy grins stretching from one ear to the other. Confetti rained down onto the heads of the newlyweds like the soft sprinkling of snow.

I watched without seeing as this unfolded before me, sometimes being pushed in front of the camera with others, though I could not find the warm, glowing smile that the photographer expected. I was about to hurry off, taking my low self-esteem away, when I saw Brendan and Paula move towards me. I looked around for an escape route, but Brendan grasped my arm. They must have known that my turning up was only to inflict pain and ruin their magical day.

"Hi, Steve, so glad you could come." The bridegroom smiled at me.

Paula stood by his side and I instinctively looked away. "I'm sorry we couldn't send you an invitation, but we didn't know how to contact you, we're delighted you could make it." The words were encouraging, but the tone was flat and unconvincing.

Brendan took her hand to lead her away. "I do hope you'll come to the reception."

"We'll be there," I heard Angela say as if from a distance.

The rest of the evening was a blur, except the moment when Matt Bishop moved towards me and shook my hand. As he talked, the vision of him raising his arm as I pulled back the sledgehammer filled my head, blitzing out any possibility of words from me. I attempted a smile and moved on. As soon as I deemed it acceptable, I elected to leave, but Angela appeared at my side.

"I think you should stay with me tonight?" she suggested. "I don't mean anything untoward – you can sleep on the sofa." I saw the concern in her eyes. "You look in a bad way, I don't think you're in any fit state to drive back to Bridgwater. You need to be with someone."

I collapsed onto Angela's sofa, though sleep was out of the question. I tossed and turned, my mind full of questions that I couldn't answer. It was no good, I had to know. I pushed the blanket to one side, went upstairs and shook Angela awake. "Why are you spying on me and who for?"

"Wh- what? What are you on about? What time is it?"

"Is it Jason or Brendan?"

"Steve, this is why I suggested staying, because you're losing it. There is no one you trust or can talk to about things and that's what you need right now. Can we have a coffee and talk? Put the kettle on and I'll be down in a minute."

Chapter 59

Angela

I watched as Brendan moved towards Steve, clutching his wedding album. "Is this you?" he asked aggressively, staring at the photo of well-dressed, smiley characters, except, that is, for the person Brendan was pointing at.

Steve looked awkward as he nodded.

Brendan laughed. "That seems a lifetime ago instead of twelve months ago today. You're a different person altogether." He placed his finger on his chin and gazed into the sky. "Now, I wonder what caused the change, or should I say, who?"

The awkwardness disappeared as Steve reached over and took my hand in his, his eyes warm and loving. My thoughts drifted back to that early morning when he shook me awake. "Who are you spying for?" he had demanded.

"Can we have a coffee and talk?" I had suggested, and talk we did until darkness turned to light and uncertainty turned to a warm understanding of one another. We found we both had a difficult early life, though Steve's was far worse than mine. I grew up without a father and didn't realise that I was illegitimate with a half-brother until I was twenty-one. Steve's childhood made mine seem normal. Handed over from one adoptive parent to another, then passed back to his real parents, who were in a strange, sexless marriage. As he explained, the first adult that he looked up to and respected was Gordon Davies, which is why he found the mental disintegration and early demise of his mentor so hard to swallow. He was right, though; Brendan had sent me to keep an eye on him on his wedding day as he knew Steve had evil plans to destroy the day.

"Angela," Brendan continued, "I said, have you two set a date yet?"

I looked lovingly at my fiancé and then at the shining ring on my finger. "Not yet, but soon."

"Oh, no hurry, then?"

"We're happy and that's the important thing."

My mind returned once more to that most important day of my life. Steve had left after our early-morning sharing of our early life and problems and I assumed he had returned to Bridgwater. It seemed that I had barely collapsed on the sofa when the phone rang.

"Can we meet up for lunch?" Steve had asked without any preamble.

"Where are you? Aren't you on the way home?"

"No, I've being walking up the hills."

I returned to the present when I became aware of Matt Bishop in front of Steve and me, wearing a big smile. "I've got a very special guest who has travelled an amazing distance, just to see you."

Steve looked at me and shrugged. "I've no idea."

"Follow me," instructed Matt, and there, standing talking to Emily was Liz Davies. As she watched us approach, her eyes lit up.

"Steve, congratulations, and you must be Angela." She hugged us both. "Jason phoned me and told me about your engagement and this party. I just had to come. There is no way I could miss it."

I studied the gentle face of the woman in front of me. The lines at the corners of her eyes were pronounced, but there was an undoubted openness about her warm smile that spoke of her goodness.

Steve took my hand. "I'm so sorry Angela, I know I've spoken many times of Liz, but I should introduce you properly. Liz is – I don't know what to say – she's been like a mother to me."

The smile disappeared as Liz turned her head to look behind her. "Perhaps second mother might be better."

Steve laughed, before Liz continued. "Your mother is here."

Steve looked confused. "Sorry, what did you say?"

"She's here."

"In this country?"

"No, she's here, in the next room," said Liz.

I watched as his hand went to his mouth, his eyes wide. He looked around, unsure where to go.

"Steve? Are you all right?" I reached for his hand.

"No, I…"

Chapter 60

Steve

My legs felt leaden as I followed Liz away from the noise towards the next room. The lightness and happiness that had surrounded my fiancée and me had disappeared and now I felt I was entering a funeral where the deceased would be put in a furnace. I was the deceased.

"I'll leave you," said Liz with an encouraging smile as she pushed open the door.

There in front of me stood my parents, who should have offered me unreserved love and affection when I was growing up. Instead I had been a burden they preferred to be without. I took a sharp intake of breath and turned back towards the door, letting go of Angela's hand.

"Steven! Don't go, I have to talk to you!"

I looked back at the grey-haired woman with the beseeching expression.

"Please! I know I treated you badly, but I need to explain. Please?"

"It's important. You must listen," said my father in the voice I remembered without fondness.

Confused, I looked towards Angela and took her hand once more. She nodded and we moved towards the chairs.

My mother coughed. "We haven't always been truthful with you," she began.

"Why doesn't that surprise me?" I blurted out angrily.

"Steven, please, I know this is difficult for you, but it's painful for me as well." She coughed again and took a sip of her drink before continuing. "There's no easy way to tell you this, so here goes. Dan is not your real father."

I gasped. "You mean all these years, you've led me to believe that he is?" – I pointed at Dan – "And it's all a pack of lies. So, who is my father? What happened to him?"

My mother looked down, unable to face either me or, as I later realised, that brutal time that she forced herself to remember. "The man I had been together with for a long time and thought I was in love with, turned out to be a brutal, violent bully."

Coldness filled the room as she tried to keep her emotions under control. "When I was pregnant with you, he beat me really, really badly before leaving for good. It was a miracle you survived. So no, I will never tell you his name, he deserves no part of your life." She sniffed and pulled out her handkerchief.

I was stunned. "Do I look like him?"

She looked me in the eye. "It has taken me years to wipe everything about that bastard from my mind. I have forced myself to forget what he looks like, sounds like, or anything about him. Please, this is so painful."

I noticed the gentle trickle of tears and looked away, feeling decidedly uncomfortable. Did not knowing who my true father was make any difference to my life? Not a jot. Did my mother's deceit make any difference to my life? Never. Did I feel any pity for the pain and sadness in her early life? Unexpectedly, yes, very much so.

The tears grew stronger. "After you were born, I was in a really bad place – so bad I was deemed incapable of looking after you. The beatings also made it impossible for me to trust a man in a proper relationship." She studied her glass, before taking a huge gulp. "We are not suited in many ways, but Dan has been the best friend anyone could wish for. We're together for always, aren't we dear?"

Dan smiled. "Always."

"When you eventually came back to me, I was a lousy mother. I couldn't love you like I should, I just couldn't. I kept seeing that evil face."

I saw Angela's expression, which held an encouraging look that I recognised.

"But when Jason phoned me and told me about your engagement, I was so excited and happy for you. Dan and I had to come and offer our congratulations, face to face. Angela, I can see you are a lovely person. I know you will be very happy together and I'm over the moon for you both."

I felt emotion threatening to overflow as I moved towards my mother and embraced her. "Thanks so much for travelling all this way, and more importantly, explaining about things. I understand now why things were so difficult. Today is a new start, and as soon as we have set a date for the wedding, you will be the first person I tell."

She hugged me to her, unwilling to let go. I gently moved away. "We'll talk later, but I need to socialise now. Let me introduce you to some of the others."

We walked out of the room and joined the milling crowd. "I ought to introduce you to the owners of this fine establishment. Here they are. Emily, meet my mum."

Chapter 61

Emily

Liz had phoned me before the party and asked if it was okay for Dan and Tracy to come. She wasn't aware of that horrific day when they abducted Paula, or the way in which they had pretended to be friends simply to infiltrate their way into my life. The thought of seeing Dan and Tracy in person made me shudder. But I had talked it over with Matt and we decided to be as friendly and agreeable as possible for the sake of this special day, and put the past behind us. Despite that, even forewarned, when their faces came towards me I felt a surge of loathing, but I quickly held out my hand and beamed a big, broad, toothy smile. "How lovely to see you both. Thank you for taking the trouble to travel all the way from Cyprus. Let me introduce Brendan. Paula you met briefly many years ago."

They looked cowed, then Uncle Matt appeared at my side. "Heh, we need smiles and laughter – glum faces are not allowed today. It's a special day for these two young'uns. It's their first of lots and lots of wedding anniversaries as well as a celebration of Steve and Angela's engagement."

"Oh no, it's Beverley," Paula sighed.

"Hello, everyone." Conversations ground to a halt. "Hello." People turned towards the slim blonde girl with the radiant smile standing on a chair. "As this is a special day for my sister, I felt I should say a few words."

"That's more than enough," groaned Paula.

"As she is my older sister, I have had to care for her and get her out of many scrapes over the years, but this time last year, Brendan took over this most challenging of tasks, which he has performed most admirably. I have to say…"

"*No, you don't!*" shouted Paula.

"…In our early, difficult years," continued Beverley as a serious expression clouded her face, "she looked after me like a wonderful junior parent and I will always love her to bits."

She stepped down off the chair and Paula reached over and pulled her into her arms. Quietness filled the room before the partygoers broke into enthusiastic clapping.

Brendan held up his hand to silence the gathering. "I would like to share with you some thoughts on my wonderful half-sister that I never knew I had until three years ago." He coughed. "Can you imagine someone you have never seen before, knocking on your door, and with very little preamble announcing themselves as your sister? How many people would have the courage to do that? She did, and over the next few months when I was going through a difficult time, she was like a rock – always there for me, offering support." He lifted a glass of champagne to his lips. "Thank you, Angela – you're a star."

I was about to walk away when I saw Dan slowly get to his feet with both arms aloft to get attention. "Please?"

His hair was a little greyer but he still had that calm, friendly expression that I had wrongly perceived as being reassuring all those years ago.

"Many of you don't know who I am." He paused. "And those who do, wish they didn't."

There was a gentle titter from those who thought he was joking.

Fear coursed through me. "*Matt, what's he going to say? What lies is he going to come out with now?*"

"I'm here to celebrate my stepson – Steven – and Angela's

engagement. Though his mother, Tracy, and I have not been in touch with him for many years, we are delighted – no, more than that, we are over the moon – that he has found love and happiness." He raised his glass. "Thank you, Angela. You are a very special lady." He looked nervously towards Liz Davies. "As some of you know, my brother was Gordon Davies, who, after a really bad chapter in his life, found God, and equally life-changing, he found Liz. Gordon became the most incredibly kind, generous and supportive person anyone could possibly wish to meet."

I looked around to see that the laughter had disappeared and everyone's gaze was fixed firmly on him.

"The bad chapter in his life was when he was sent to prison. He accepted it and believed it to be God's will. I couldn't accept it. Later when he was hit by that horror of all horror's, Parkinson's, he accepted that as well; he believed it to be his rightful punishment for the wrongs he had committed in his earlier life. I couldn't accept it." His eyes turned down towards the floor. "Then as death became inevitable, he coped, and thanked God for his wonderful proper life. I should explain, he believed that his life only started when he found the Lord. Me, I hated God and hated everyone and everything and in particular one family." He turned towards Matt.

"That's the reason I'm standing here." He paused. "It's to humbly apologise for the pain and distress I have inflicted either by myself or through others. I was very, very wrong."

He moved towards Matt and held out his hand. With a big grin, Matt grabbed it warmly. The gathering watched and slowly the laughter and noise returned as I put my arm through my husband's. Dan held up his hand then continued. "After talking to Steve and Jason as well as what I have seen myself, it is clear the Bishop family are incredible and one that Gordon would have be proud to know."

*

When Matt and I were cuddled up together in bed later, he murmured, "Do you remember all those years ago at junior school, when I had a certain problem and all those kids were chasing me?"

I laughed.

"I turned and punched the first person I saw in the eye, and it was you?"

"I do."

He kissed me. "Careful about saying that – you made that mistake before."

I laughed again.

"Well," he said seriously, "it was the best thing I ever did."

I punched him gently in the ribs. "But it was me who phoned you after you'd been sent home."

"Yes, but it was me who suggested meeting up on the way to school."

We both laughed, then Matt spoke softly. "We were always meant to be, it's as simple as that."

It was a long time before we fell asleep.

Chapter 62

Matt

The week following our party we received countless messages by text or email or even the old-fashioned telephone saying what a superb evening it had been and how much it had been enjoyed. For Emily, Paula, Beverley and me, it had a deeper significance than enjoyment. We all knew that Steve and Jason had long ago turned the corner, and we now thought of them as close friends, almost family. But the speech by Dan was not so much closing a chapter – more like throwing a book in the fire and writing the prologue for the next. The next was definitely going to be happier than the first horror story. I knew Dan and Tracy were due to return to Cyprus in a couple of days and was desperate to show that I recognised the enormity of what he had said.

"What d'you think, Em, about a sort of family meal out?"

"Sounds good. What's the problem?"

"Why d'you think there is a problem?" I inquired.

"Because you've been mulling it over for hours, dearest."

I laughed. "I can't get away with anything, can I?"

"Never. So, what are you worried about, tell me."

So, I told her I was thinking off inviting Dan, Tracy, Steve and Angela, Jason and Margaret as well as the obvious, Paula and Brendan and Beverley and her latest, Gavin I think it was.

"Excellent idea," said Emily with a kiss. "It sort of puts a definite line under the 'Dastardly Davieses Debacle'."

"That's my thinking."

*

"Ah, Mr Bishop, I believe," said the concierge.

"That's right. We've booked a table for twelve."

"We're a bit early," muttered Beverley.

"Perfect, follow me." The dark suit and fixed smile led us to our table where we sat, boy, girl, boy, girl, with Tracy next to me. The evening started quietly, but with Beverley telling her silly stories, encouraged by Margaret and aided by the wine, the chatter and laughter got louder.

Paula's laugher suddenly stopped as she looked behind me. "Oh no, it's my boss. He's seen me – he's coming over."

A well-dressed, confident man appeared at the table. "Paula, what a nice surprise. I thought I'd come over and say hello. Hope I'm not interrupting your fun evening." A big grin spread across his face.

At the sound of the voice, Tracy's head snapped around in alarm. "*IT IS, IT'S YOU!*" Her eyes were wide and the tears began to slide down her face as she pushed her chair back. "*Get away from me!*" she shouted as he moved towards her. "*Don't you dare touch me. Call the police!*" Other diners looked across in horror as she cowered away from the smartly dressed man before rushing towards the exit, with Dan chasing after her.

The evening disintegrated with a pale-faced, dismay-stricken Simon Roach apologising profusely. "I didn't see her, honestly, I didn't. I would have left if I'd known." He immediately exited the restaurant, leaving us stunned and the evening shattered as we tried hard to ignore what had just happened and engage in a normal conversation that was not controversial. Some time later Dan phoned and checked that Roach had left before returning on his own to the muted gathering as we sipped our coffee. "Tracy was sorry for ruining the evening," he said, "and she asked me to come and explain things."

I listened to the story that Kevin had shared with me some time ago, except now I knew who the evil, vicious ex-boyfriend of

196

Tracy was. As Dan was explaining, Steve interrupted in a hoarse, disbelieving voice. "That man's my father. He is, isn't he?"

Dan nodded. "He is your biological father, yes. Tracy was adamant that you should never know who he was, but this evening's unfortunate meeting has changed things."

"So that's the man, Paula's boss, who rakes in mega money, is powerful and respectable and is the sort of person everyone looks up to." Steve paused, considering. "With his evil, violent bullying, I'm lucky to be here, lucky to be born even. He ruined my mother's life and ruined my early life and yet with his wealth and position he is God's gift to society." He stood up and turned to Angela. "I think it's time to go."

Chapter 63

Steve

That monster was my father! I tried to absorb that abhorrent thought but couldn't. The memory of his smooth face and well-spoken accent leapt into my brain and refused to go away. "Paula, what a nice surprise, I thought I'd come over and say hello." My mother had told me at the party what had happened to her when she was pregnant and the effect the violent bullying had on her, and while her story was horrifying and beggared belief, I'd had no face to put on that evil brute. Now that I did, those eyes, that smile engulfed me. They were there in front of me, and, horror of all horrors, I was part of him! He was in my genes! Had I inherited any of his traits? Could I hit Angela, the love of my life? Was it possible?

"Are you all right?" Angela had asked more than once, when we returned home and I entered a detached, unreal world oblivious to anything except HIM, the monster.

I got through that night and the following day before I put on my coat. "I won't be long," I said to Angela, before forgetting to kiss her goodbye for the first time ever.

"Where are you going?" she asked, her strained voice echoing the look of concern. "You're going to see him, aren't you?"

I opened the door.

"Steve, don't do anything silly. You're in a good place now, don't ruin everything, *PLEASE*," she shouted as I pushed the door shut, my hand gripping the knuckleduster lying in my pocket. I had coerced Roach's address from Jason, who had been to a works do with Paula, some time ago at his house.

I rang the doorbell and within seconds that face loomed before me.

I just about managed to croak out, "I'd like a few words with you," as he raised his arm to show me into the lounge, seemingly unsurprised at my being there.

"You're one of the party from last night, aren't you?" He spoke in that already irritatingly confident voice.

I nodded, as he studied me.

"You're one of Tracy's lads, aren't you?"

"Yeah, the only one," I forced out as I tried to control the hatred that was burning through my body while my grip tightened on the knuckleduster in my pocket.

Then I watched the colour disappear from his face and his smile slide away. "How old are you?" he murmured.

"Why?" I growled.

"You are, aren't you? You're my son?"

"If you mean did you provide the sperm, the answer's 'yes'." I lifted the weapon from my pocket, anger raging.

He looked at my hand then his eyes lifted to stare at my face as tears flowed down his cheeks.

"*My son.*" His eyes lit up as he moved towards me.

"Don't you dare touch me. You ruined my life, my mother's life, and you live a life of luxury, you bastard."

"*My son!*"

I shouted angrily, "Don't you ever refer to me as your son again! You're an ogre, you don't exist." I found myself caressing the knuckleduster in my hand. "The way you savaged my mother when she was pregnant with me means I'm lucky to be alive, lucky to be born, and you got off scot-free."

"I loved your mother, I really did." He buried his face in his hands. "Never a day goes by without me tearing myself apart for what I did. I will never forgive myself, never."

"So, why were you a vicious, evil bully?" I kept clenching and unclenching my fist.

"It's no excuse, but my father wanted me to join his business in finance and I was desperate to pursue my love for art. We argued about it constantly, but when Tracy became pregnant, I knew I had no choice. I took to drugs to deal with it and, and…" His sobbing left me cold as I studied my metal fist.

"I never want to see you again, but I'll leave you with a gift to remember me by." I drew back my fist before throwing the knuckleduster on the floor between his feet and left to the sound of uncontrollable weeping.

No sooner had I pushed the key in the door, when it was flung open and Angela fell into my arms.

"You didn't do anything silly, did you? Please, tell me you didn't? Steve, answer me. You didn't hit him?"

I pulled her to me. "I nearly did. I so nearly beat the daylights out of him, but then I thought in a strange way it would somehow make him feel better, as if punishment would allow him to move on; so I couldn't. Besides, why on earth should I ruin this wonderful life with the love of my life, to be no better than that monster?"

Chapter 64

Paula

"I can't do it. I can't go to work and look that monster in the eye and do whatever he tells me, when I know what he did to Tracy. I can't do it."

Brendan put his arm around me and kissed me on the cheek. "Look, love, I'll call in sick for you tomorrow and that will give you time to decide what to do – whether to stay or go. There's no point in staying if you're fretting about it all the time."

When my phone rang late afternoon I was surprised to see it was Brian James! What was going on? He had never phoned me at home before.

"Sorry to bother you, Paula, but something has come up. I'd like you to come here, to Bromsgrove, first thing tomorrow – it's important."

"What's it about, Brian?"

"Splendid. See you eight thirty. Have a good evening."

I put the phone down on the table.

"Who was it, love? You look lost in another world."

I paused, trying to return to normality. "It was Brian James, my old boss at Bromsgrove. He wants to see me tomorrow morning."

"So, why d'you look so worried?"

Why was I worried. Why? Then the light dawned. "Doesn't it strike you as odd that the day after that debacle at Brown's, I'm called in?" I took Brendan's hand. "There I was, unsure if I could face

Roach ever again and he's either sent me back to work in Bromsgrove, or…or he's arranged for Brian James to sack me. That's it, he's made up some lies that he's fed to James and got him to do the dirty work."

I felt the warm arms envelope me. "Just stay calm. Let's enjoy the evening and try to put tomorrow to one side. Now, what can we do?"

I arrived at Walker Investments, Bromsgrove, half an hour early but sat in my car until 8.20am when I strode purposefully towards the building.

"Hi, Paula. Good to see you again." Brian James's secretary gave me a warm smile as she ushered me into his office.

"Paula, take a seat. Would you like coffee?"

I shook my head. "No thanks." I just wanted this meeting over and done with. I looked at my old boss. His expression was unusually serious.

"No doubt you're curious about why you are here?"

The question didn't need an answer. He paused, then lifted the cup to his lips, before continuing. "Last night just before I rang you, I received a call from Simon."

This was it – this was the lies followed by my marching orders. I tensed, ready to shout out my denial, and refute everything thrown at me.

"He's leaving Walker Investments today and is saying goodbye to the rest of the workforce this morning. A bit sudden, to say the least, but he was insistent, even though it was against the terms of his contract, but we will get by, we always do."

I slumped back in my seat as I tried to take this on board.

"But he was adamant about what should happen to you. He felt you should move back here."

I wasn't being sacked then, not yet – just booted out again.

"I agreed with him, so I'm replacing him in Birmingham and I'd like you to take over from me here."

I gasped. "You want me to be CEO here?"

"That's right. We can sort out the money side later, but be sure it will be significantly more than you are currently getting. Is that okay – you don't look too sure?"

I leapt out of my chair, and to his surprise, kissed him on the cheek. "That's wonderful, I couldn't be happier."

"Excellent, excellent. I'll speak to Simon and arrange for your stuff to be sent over here." His broad, engaging smile had returned as he stood up.

I had to ask. "Just one thing, Brian. What's Simon Roach going to do?"

He shrugged. "He's leaving the area, leaving financial investment and doing something he's always wanted to do, apparently – whatever that is."

"So, it's not all bad then, oh ye of little faith," said Brendan when I returned home from work.

"It's acceptable," I replied with a huge grin. "I must phone Bev and tell her.

I dialled her number.

"That's wonderful – well deserved. Are you going round to Uncle Matt to give them the news?" she inquired.

"I thought I would. Are you coming?"

"Uh, yes please. Can you pick me up?"

I'm ashamed to say that I was so wrapped up in my own small world that I didn't notice that my usually lively sister was strangely quiet.

"You sounded very excited on the phone," said Uncle Matt.

"I've got some marvellous news!"

"You are, aren't you – you're pregnant!" shouted Emily, leaping up from her chair and hugging me.

"No, I'm not. We are trying and it will happen, it will." I felt the euphoria of my news ebb away, but aided by a glass of wine, the laughter returned and I told them of my work promotion. There were hearty congratulations and more wine. Then Emily turned to Beverley. "You're unusually quiet. Is anything wrong?"

We watched in amazement as her face crumpled and her eyes filled with tears. "I am, I'm pregnant."

Chapter 65

Matt

The room went quiet as we absorbed Beverley's revelation, then Emily put her arms around her. "Darling, that's wonderful, wonderful news."

"Is it?" She brushed away the tears and looked at her sister for her reaction.

Paula reached over and kissed Bev on the cheek. "I'm really pleased for you, Sis."

"But how can you be? You are desperate for children and I'm not even sure whether I'm ready to be a mother, or whether I want this child."

"You're not, are you?" exclaimed Paula. "You're not going to abort it, are you? That's awful. It's evil. It's the worst kind of murder imaginable."

"Paula, please, I'm not thinking rationally," she sobbed. "I only found out I was up the duff a week ago and I can't take it in."

I turned towards Emily but she was in a state of shock. I couldn't sit on the fence, whether it was the right thing to do or not. "Bev, you're upset. It's a huge shock, but you need to give yourself time. It's a decision that's going to shape the rest of your life. What about the father, have you told him yet?"

"Gavin, no. I don't know how to approach him, what to say." She looked like a child, lost and afraid. I pulled her to me with Emily by my side. "I don't know if he'll be pleased or not."

The ring of the doorbell broke the spell. "I'll go," shouted Paula.

"I hope we're not interrupting anything," said Dan as he entered the room.

"We were passing, saw your car in the drive, and as we're going back home tomorrow we thought we would pop in and say cheerio," Tracy added.

"That's so good of you." I kissed Tracy on the cheek before shaking Dan's hand. "We were just celebrating Paula's promotion. Would you like a glass of wine?" I saw Tracy study Beverley's tear-smitten face with concern.

"Perfect timing," said Beverley brightly. "I can't cope with all this stupid banter, it brings tears to my eyes. Excuse me, I need to go to the bathroom."

Emily returned with a bottle of Rioja, which she poured liberally.

"I know I've said this before, but I can never say it enough times: I'm really sorry for all the hurt I've caused and thank you all for being so understanding," said Dan.

This was accompanied by a firm nod of the head by Tracy, who continued: "In particular to you Paula, for that dreadful, dreadful day when we used you to get at the Bishop family. There's no excusing such an evil act." I watched Paula study her shoes as she avoided any eye contact.

Dan broke into the awkward silence. "I want you to know that any time you want a break, you are always welcome to stay with us in Paphos."

"And if we're not there, you can stay anyway," Tracy laughed.

When Beverley returned from the bathroom, I left her and Paula to entertain our guests while Emily and I went into the kitchen to put some nibbles together. "They seem very happy," murmured Emily. "Is it because they're leaving, d'you think?"

We placed the dishes on the dining table as Tracy turned to us. "We were just saying, we popped in to see Steven and Angela earlier. Steven told us that he had been to see That Man and now he could put him to one side and move on. My everlasting regret is that I couldn't be the mother I wanted to be and watch and help him grow up. It's the greatest moment of one's life and I missed it."

Dan stroked her arm. "Well, I reckon it won't be too long before Steve and Angela have children and we're hoping they have lots of holidays in Cyprus."

I looked across at Beverley, concerned for her reaction to the baby talk, but the warm, lively expression was back.

We were sorry to see our visitors leave – something none of us thought we would ever experience. "Well," I inquired, "what d'you think?"

Paula answered first. "I thought I was coming round here to celebrate my promotion, but that news has been firmly put in its rightful place at the bottom of the front page."

Emily spoke next. "I know we've only met Gavin once, but we liked him, didn't we?"

She looked at me for confirmation.

"We did. Compared with some of your other boyfriends he seemed, how can I put it?"

"Grown-up?" suggested Beverley. "You're right. Some of the others I've known just wanted arm candy. As soon as I first met him in the art materials shop, I knew he was different." She gave a half-hearted laugh. "He cost me a fortune, because I kept going back buying stuff I didn't need just to see him. Eventually he got the message and asked me out. I could see straight away he was different. He was interested in me, my work, what I wanted from life – grown-up stuff."

"Then you need to be grown-up and talk to him," said Emily.

I watched Beverley's face begin to crumble again. "But what if he thinks I've tried to nail him? I've got pregnant just to force him into marriage like a real evil, conniving cow?"

"You need to trust him, Bev. Trust your own instincts that he's a good person." I hugged her to me. I had never seen her so down and lost. "D'you want to stay here tonight?"

She shook her head. "I need to go."

"If you need to talk?" suggested Emily.

Chapter 66

Matt

Paula left not long after Beverley, and I was in deep conversation with Emily, not surprisingly about Beverley and her future, when the doorbell chimed.

"I bet that's Bev. She's made a decision before she even got home, and she's come back to tell us," said Emily.

I went to the door, but it wasn't Bev. It was a young man with worry lines across his face. It was Gavin.

"I've been trying to get hold of Bev, but she's not answering her phone. I thought perhaps she might be here?" He tried to sound relaxed, but the concern was evident.

"You just missed her, Gavin, but she should be back home by now." Emily gave a warm smile. "Would you like a drink of anything?"

"No, thank you. I'd better be going." He retreated to the door, then turned back. "I hope you don't mind me asking, but is everything all right with Bev, only she doesn't seem herself."

I looked at Emily, seeking guidance. "You two need to talk, Gavin. Don't put it off," she said firmly.

I watched his shoulders slump. "What's going on?"

"Please, talk as soon as possible," I confirmed.

"Why? What's so important? What is it she's not telling me?"

"Talk to her, Gavin," Emily and I reiterated in unison.

Things were getting too complicated, too stressful and it was made worse the following morning when Paula appeared at the door on her way to work. Emily and I had only just surfaced and we were not ready for what was thrown our way.

Paula grabbed a cup of coffee then sat opposite, barely suppressed excitement shining from her face as she lifted her drink then placed it back on the table untouched.

"After Bev's revelation last night, it got me thinking and I wondered what your thoughts are." She looked at Emily.

"Go on," said Emily.

"Well, she said that she wasn't ready to be a mother, which I understand. So, if she gives birth, I could, I could perhaps adopt it."

Emily took her hand. "Paula, I know how hard this is for you, I really do. But Beverley is still trying to come to terms with what is probably the most important decision of her life. Give her time."

Paula's eyes looked pleadingly at Emily. "But it could be the answer, couldn't it?"

Before she could respond, she leapt into the air at the sound of the hammering on the door. "My God, it's like Paddington Station this morning."

It was Beverley and Gavin, who strode in wearing huge grins.

"I think you've talked," said Emily, smiling.

"We have and Gavin's over the moon, aren't you darling?" Beverley kissed her boyfriend.

"So, you're ready to be a mother, then, Bev?" asked Paula gently.

"I am, and Gavin is ready to be a father. We're ready to be a family. Isn't it wonderful?" She jumped up and down in excitement, before she realised. "Oh, gosh, Paula, I forgot."

"Don't, Bev. This is your day. I'm really, really happy for you. You'll be a great mother, I know you will."

I watched as Beverley pulled her sister to her and hugged her with tears in her eyes.

"Right," I said. "We need to drink a toast to the parents-in-waiting. I'm afraid it's too early for alcohol, so coffee will have to do."

"Hear, hear!" shouted Paula. "You need to give some thought to names. Bartholomew or Cassandra," she suggested with a broad smile.

"It needs to be something that goes with his or her surname," said Emily. "If it's Carr you can't call him Parker."

"Or if it's Thyme, you can't call her Rosemary," added Paula.

"So, what is your surname?" I asked. "Sorry, I don't know it."

Beverley interrupted. "It's too early to be thinking about names. Anyway, that's our news. Are you excited about your new job, Sis?"

"Davies," said Gavin. "Gavin Davies."

Cold silence invaded the room, leaving a confused Gavin looking towards Beverley.

"Anyway, that's our news," said Beverley, studying her watch. "We'd better be going."

I had to know. "Where are you from, Gavin? Which part of the country?"

"I'm from Kidderminster, why?"

"You're not related to Gordon Davies or Dan Davies?" I rushed out.

"No, look, what's going on?" There was a hint of anger.

"D'you know a Tracy Davies or Steve…"

"Beverley, why am I being interrogated like this?"

Beverley had her hand across her mouth but when she took it away, the huge smile metamorphosed into uncontrollable laughter.

We all stared at her in amazement, before her infectious nature made everyone join in, including Gavin though he didn't have a clue why she was laughing.

"Yes?" I invited when she eventually stopped.

"Sorry, it's just that when Dan and Tracy were here last night, they were our new best friends, almost family. They even invited us over there. But it's the name DAVIES that's synonymous with everything bad that has happened to us and instantly puts you on high alert."

"Um, I think she's right," said Emily, looking at me.

"So, I think my new baby shall be called Cassandra Bishop-Davies, or Bartholomew Davies-Bishop, not sure which."

"Bev, you need to explain," suggested her boyfriend.

"Sorry Gavin, it's a long story and I'll tell you everything when we get home."

Chapter 67

Emily

Beverley was a different person after the birth of Cassie Bishop Davies. Change was inevitable, but the bright sparkling eyes had slightly faded and the high-energy, never-stay-still girl had gone. Now there was a sense of serenity, of inner peace that engulfed her like a shroud. The paints and canvasses were put to one side, no longer important. Whenever she gazed at Cassie her face had a look of wonder. Matt and I understood after the gift from God that was Harry, but at least we had got used to bringing up Paula and Beverley albeit as surrogate parents. Beverley was in a new, wondrous world.

Paula gave birth to a baby boy only six months later. When she first turned up with Brendan and blurted out, "I am, I really am, I'm pregnant!" she seemed to alternate between unbelievable excitement and fear as she danced from foot to foot. How would she cope if anything went wrong? But she did cope, by packing in the job that she had longed for and moving carefully around, watching what she ate and simply living from moment to moment. When she gave birth, she was euphoric.

Paula and Beverley came round every Sunday with Bart and Cassie. Brendan and Gavin dropped them off before they put parenthood to one side and disappeared to the pub where they would chat about football, work, politics – anything other than babies. When they returned, the rapture on their faces made it clear where their hearts truly lay.

"Remember when we collected Paula and Beverley from their grandparents?" asked Matt one Sunday evening as we lay in bed.

"Of course, it was a life-changing day," I replied as a broad smile spread across my face. "Why have you mentioned it now?"

"It's just that when I see them now as new parents with the joy on their faces and think back to the uncertainty with Paula at that time, how she was a real madam—"

I interrupted. "It was only because she thought she would be unfaithful to her real mother if she showed me any affection."

"I know," continued Matt, "and before then the Davieses were doing their best to wreak havoc."

"Don't I know it. Trying to get me thrown out of my teaching job and getting that Judy Sayers to seduce you."

"Attempting and failing," he said, as he leaned over and kissed me.

"Then they kidnapped Paula on that awful, awful day."

"And they came up with their lies to tear Paula and Bev apart, amongst other things," I chimed in. "Matt, where are you going with this?"

"It's just that whenever anyone mentions the name Davies, I feel this evil dark cloud descend on me."

"I know. I'll always remember your expression when Gavin told us his surname was Davies," I laughed. "It was a real picture."

"But that's just it," said my darling husband. "Now for the first time in twenty-five years, when the word Davies is uttered, I think of baby Cassie. I think of that lovely, adorable baby and I can't stop smiling. The Dastardly Davieses are gone for ever."

"Hurray!" I concluded. "Amen."

Lightning Source UK Ltd.
Milton Keynes UK
UKHW010800250821
389444UK00003B/430